THE COMPROMISE

THE COMPROMISE

by Sergei Dovlatov

Translated from the Russian
by Anne Frydman

CHATTO & WINDUS
THE HOGARTH PRESS
LONDON

First published in 1983 by
Chatto & Windus · The Hogarth Press
40 William IV Street, London WC2N 4DF

All rights reserved. No part of this publication may be reproduced, stored in a retrieval system, or transmitted in any form, or by any means, electronic, mechanical, photocopying, recording or otherwise, without the prior permission of the publisher.

British Library Cataloguing in Publication Data
Dovlatov, Sergei
 The compromise
 I. Title II. Kompromiss. *English*
 891.73'44 [F]   PG3479.6.O85

 ISBN 0–7011–2756–2
 ISBN 0–7011–2757–0 Pbk

Translation Copyright © 1983 by Alfred A. Knopf, Inc.
Copyright © 1981 by Sergei Dovlatov

Originally published as *Kompromiss* by Silver Age Publishing, New York.
"The Fifth Compromise," published as "Jubilee Boy," and "The Eighth Compromise," published as "Somebody's Death and Other Problems," originally appeared in *The New Yorker*.
Portions of this book have been previously published in *Grand Street*, *Partisan Review* and the *Columbia Journalism Review*.

The translator wishes to acknowledge, with deep gratitude, the invaluable help of Rose Raskin. Any mistakes have been despite her efforts.

Published in Great Britain by
Richard Clay (The Chaucer Press) Ltd,
Bungay, Suffolk

To my mother, N. S. Dovlatova—
for everything she's gone through!

THE COMPROMISE

. . . So I found myself without work. Maybe, I thought, I should learn to be a tailor? I've noticed that tailors are always in a good mood.

I met Loginov, who works at the television studio.

"Greetings. How are things?"

"Well, like this: I'm looking for work."

"I know where there's a vacancy. The newspaper *On Watch for the Motherland*. Take down this name: Kashirin."

"A bald-headed guy, right?"

"Kashirin is an experienced journalist. As a person, rather soft."

"Muck is also soft," I said.

"What, you know him?"

"No."

"Then what are you going on about? Write down his name."

I wrote it down.

"You should get dressed up to see him. My wife says, if you just get properly dressed . . ."

His wife, by the way, once happened to call me up . . . Stop! That opens up a broad, disturbing topic that would take us too far off the track.

"When I make some money, I'll get properly dressed. I'll buy a top hat."

I gathered together newspaper clippings of pieces I had written. Picked out the most worthwhile.

I didn't like Kashirin. A lackluster face, army sense of humor. After one look at me he said, "You're not a Party member, of course?"

I shook my head guiltily. With a kind of idiotic simple-mindedness he added, "There were about twenty candidates for this job. They come talk to me . . . and don't show up again after that. At least leave me your telephone number."

I gave him the telephone number of a dry-cleaner's which for some reason had stuck in my mind.

At home I unfolded the clippings. I reread some of them, started thinking . . .

Yellowed pages. Ten years of lies and dissembling. And yet, some people stood behind them: conversations, feelings, things that actually happened. Not on the pages themselves, but beyond them.

It's a hard road from the reported facts to the truth.

You can never step into the same river twice. But looking down through the thickness of the water you can make out the river bottom covered with tin cans. And behind magnificent theatrical decorations you can learn to see the brick wall, the ropes, the fire-extinguisher, and the drunken stagehands. All this is well known to anyone who has been behind the scenes, even if only once.

I'll start with an insignificant news brief.

THE FIRST COMPROMISE

("Soviet Estonia." November 1973.)
SCIENTIFIC CONFERENCE. Scholars of eight countries are in Tallinn for the Seventh Annual Conference on the Study of Scandinavia and Finland. There are specialists representing the USSR, Poland, Hungary, East Germany, Finland, Sweden, Denmark, and West Germany. At the conference, panel discussions on six different topics will be held. More than 130 scholars are expected to attend. Historians, archaeologists, and linguists will deliver papers and read reports. The conference will last until November 16.

The conference took place at the Polytechnic Institute. I dropped by, talked to a few people. Within five minutes I had all the information I needed for a news item. I left the piece at the secretariat. Chief Editor Turonok appeared in my office, an unctuous, marzipanish person. A certain type: the timid manipulator. On this occasion, highly excited. "You have committed a gross ideological blunder."

"?"

"You listed the countries . . ."

"That's not permitted?"

"It's permitted and necessary. The problem is the way you listed them—the order you put them in. You have here Hungary, East Germany, Denmark, then Poland, the USSR, West Germany . . ."

"Naturally, in alphabetical order."

"But that's a non-class approach," Turonok groaned. "An ironclad order must be followed. The People's Democracies—first! Then the neutral states. And at the rear the members of the capitalist bloc."

"*O kay*," I said.

I rewrote the story, gave it back to the secretariat. The next day Turonok burst into my office holding a freshly printed newspaper. "Are you trying to make a fool of me? Have you done this on purpose?"

"What is it?"

"You've mixed up the People's Democracies! You've put East Germany after Hungary! Again alphabetical order? Forget that opportunistic expression! You're a worker on a Party newspaper. Hungary goes third! They had an uprising there."

"And Germany fought a war against us."

"Don't argue! Why are you arguing with me? That was the other Germany, the other one! I can't understand it. Who trusted you? Political myopia! Moral infantilism! We'll have to raise the question . . ."

I was paid two rubles for the article. I had been sure they would pay three.

THE SECOND COMPROMISE

("Soviet Estonia." June 1974.)
RIVALS OF THE WIND (The Tallinn Hippodrome celebrates its fiftieth anniversary). Well-known jockeys, idols of the public—first and foremost they are experienced livestock specialists who persistently and patiently perfect a breed, developing valuable hereditary traits in their "pupils." In addition, they are highly qualified sportsmen who once a week validate their successes before the exacting Tallinn public. Over the past fifty years, these sportsmen have won more than a few prizes and citations, and in 1969 Master Jockey Anton Dukalski, riding the stallion Tal'nik, won the Grand All-Union Prize. Among the stars of the Tallinn Hippodrome, the most experienced and distinguished are L. Jurgens, E. Ilves, Kh. Nimmiste. The young sportsman A. Ivanov shows great promise.

To commemorate the jubilee, there will be a special racing gala held at the Hippodrome on August 1.

The Tallinn Hippodrome presents a rather dreary spectacle. A muddied oval, lopsided grandstands. The grounds littered with ticket stubs. The excited and raucous crowd circulates from the bar to the railings.

The Hippodrome is the only place where they sell port by the glass.

At the ticket window, there are two kinds of tickets to be had: "express" and "doubles." If you buy an "express," you're supposed to guess the finalists in the exact order they'll finish. For "doubles," you simply have to guess the two top winners in any order. Consequently, you're paid less for a winning "double." And the winnings are small for choosing any of the favorites. The whole Hippodrome bets on them—all the novices. The really big killings are to be had by betting on a poor horse who comes in first by chance. It's not hard to pick the favorite. It's harder to foresee the unexpected—the burst of friskiness in some mangy nag. The first-class riders can hold back the favorites if they're paid big money. To know how to lose one's place skillfully is also an art. Maybe even harder than winning. The mediocre horses really seem to be in the lead. You can sometimes win as much as 150 rubles. However, it's not likely that the good riders will have any dealings with you. They have their own steady clientele. It's simpler to come to some agreement with a third-rate jockey. He's forbidden to bet on the races himself. He has to work through a front. He will take the form for the next day's races and mark it up for you. He'll point out the top three horses in each race. And you, according to instructions, will buy tickets with a share for him.

I decided to write the jubilee notice about the Hippodrome. Conferred with its director, A. Melder. He called in the young jockey Anatoli Ivanov.

"Here," the director said, "is new talent."

Ivanov and I went off to the snack bar. I said, "I've got some spare money, about eighty rubles. What would you advise?"

"About what?"

"What I have in mind is the races."

Ivanov looked at me warily.

"Don't worry," I said. "I'm not a provocateur, even if I am a journalist."

"I'm not at all worried."

"Then what's the problem?"

The result was that he let me go in with him.

"Dukel"—that is, Dukalski—"is placing his bets through some visiting Latvians. It's a hundred percent solid operation. They take an entire race and split all the earnings. But that's at the end, when they play for high stakes. The first three races, though, can be taken."

I got the next day's racing form. Tolya pulled out a pencil.

After the third race, I was paid sixty rubles. From then on, we systematically collected thirty to eighty a day. It's a pity the races were only held once a week.

That summer, Tolya Ivanov broke a leg and a collarbone. It had nothing to do with horses. He fell out of a taxi dead drunk.

That was the end of the Hippodrome for him. For the last few years, "the rival of the wind" has been working as a bartender at the Mundi.

THE THIRD COMPROMISE

("Estonian Youth." August 1974.)
I FEEL AT HOME (Guests of Tallinn).

Alla Meleshko has an unusually attractive face. Of course, this is not the most important thing in life. And yet, and yet... it may just be the reason that everyone is so invariably well disposed to this giggling, awkward girl.

Alla is not a famous touring pop singer. She is not a participant in an advanced scientific symposium. Setting records in sports is not her domain.

Alla comes to our city... out of curiosity. Yes, yes, I mean curiosity—that disturbing feeling which causes a person to leave the safety and comfort of a native place. I would call it "the emotion of the road," the seductiveness of the horizon, the eternal restlessness of the traveler.

"In instability there is movement," wrote the famous music theoretician Czerny.

We decided to ask Alla a few questions.

"How do you like Tallinn?"

"It's a remarkable city, both cozy and austere. The harmonious contrast of the old and the modern is striking. In its quiet and calm, a proud strength can be felt."

"How do you come to be here?"

"I heard a lot about Tallinn's designers and painters. Besides, I love the sea."

"Are you traveling alone?"

"My constant companions are a camera and a volume of Aleksandr Blok's poetry."

"What have you managed to see so far?"

"Vyshgorod and Empress Catherine Park, where tame squirrels kept coming up to me, so trusting and touching."

"What are you planning further?"

"Once the summer ends, studies will begin again in my choreographic studio. Once again—dogged effort, work under pressure. But in the meantime, I feel at home here!"

In this story, there are no angels or villains. There are no sinners or saints. And there aren't any in life, either. It's been quite some time since I first observed this.

An editor once said to me, "All the people you write about are scoundrels. If your hero is a scoundrel, then by the logic of the narrative you ought to bring him to some moral catastrophe. Or else to retribution. But in your writing, scoundrels are something natural, like rain or snow."

"Where do you find any scoundrels?" I asked. "Who, for example, is a scoundrel?"

The editor looked at me the way you would look at someone who has fallen in with bad company but still tries to defend his friends.

It's a long time since I stopped dividing people into positive and negative types. And literary protagonists all the more so. Besides, I'm not at all sure that in life crimes are inevitably followed by repentance, or great deeds by bliss. We are what we sense ourselves to be. Our qualities, virtues, and vices are drawn into the light of day by the sensitive touch of life. "Thou, Nature, art my goddess! . . ." (the words of Edmund in *King Lear*, he being a scoundrel of some proportions). And so on . . . Fine . . .

In this story there are no angels or villains, and there couldn't be. One of the protagonists is me. Another is Misha Shablinsky, with his favorite expressions "spontaneous apperception" and "immanent dualism." Mitya Klensky also plays an important part, and he's easy to recognize. His passion for anodized tie-clips and heavy, fake amber cigarette holders has earned him widespread fame.

What drew the three of us together? Perhaps it would be best put as a simple hostility to the official side of newspaper work—a kind of healthy cynicism that helped us avoid pomposity.

In our office, twenty-eight of the thirty-two staff employees called themselves "Golden Pens of the Republic." We three, in order to be original, called ourselves "Silver Pens." Dima Sher, who had once written a dispatch with the line, "The artificial kidney is a commonplace phenomenon in our daily lives," was known as the "Oak Pen."

Basically, we were friends. Shablinsky worked for the Industry Desk, and his articles never provoked discussion. Statistics predominated in them; they were designed for a specific kind of reader. Klensky did a daily column for the sports department. His precise, workmanlike reporting was devoid of emotion. I wrote satirical sketches and features. The editor had said to me as early as April, "If you write satirical sketches, we'll give you an apartment."

It's not easy to do. Every fact has to be carefully checked. The targets of critical attack dodge and take cover. Our city is small, people are in the public eye. To make it short, there were two attempts to beat me up. Once it was the teamsters of a freight station (successful). The second time a currency speculator named Chigir hit me with a borsalino hat and promptly received a knockout punch in return.

My articles always provoked numerous responses from readers. Sometimes in threatening form. This even pleased me—hate signifies that the newspaper is still capable of exciting passions.

Each of us attended to his business. We didn't earn bad salaries. From his out-of-town assignments, Shablinsky would bring back dried fish, duck eggs, and even live piglets. Klensky did some ghost writing for a retired sportsman known as "the good plantation owner." In brief, we worked conscientiously and honestly.

What else? Nothing in particular. Someone from Dvinsk came to visit Mitya Klensky. I don't even know what she had in mind. There are certain young women who are not what you'd call immoral or loose, but rather, to put it better, they're carefree. Their lives are entirely composed of happenings. Behind this piling-up of actions it's sometimes hard to guess that they have souls. With horrible efforts, at the price of any sacrifice, these girls will, to give one example, provide themselves with imported boots. It's difficult to imagine just how much time and strength this requires. And later they have to parade the imported boots, at countless gatherings of friends, at dances, or simply on the walk from the department store to the town hall past the store windows. Sometimes these boots lie dark beside your bed: massive platform soles, cracked tops. And not because of any terrible immorality. It's just that they aren't married. They drank too much, the buses weren't running, they couldn't get a taxi. And the host of the party had been so nice. He had three icons in his apartment, Magomayev's signature, engravings, Cole Porter . . . Evenings the girls dance, days they work. And they don't work badly either. And they go to visit interesting people. Journalists, for example.

Mitya dropped by my office. There was a girl with him.

"Sit here," he said to her. "My chief is in a bad mood. Serge, is it all right with you if she sits here?"

I said, "It's all right."

The girl sat down by the window, pulled out a compact. Mitya left. I continued to work without any special ardor. The satirical sketch I was writing was entitled, "VMK Without Retouching." What *VMK* stands for I have completely forgotten.

"What's your name?"

"Alla Meleshko. Is it true that all journalists dream of writing a novel?"

"No," I lied.

The girl put on lipstick and started to fidget. I asked, "Where are you studying?"

At this point, she began to lie. Some dramatic studio, some

sort of pantomime, a Yugoslav director had asked her to take part in shooting some film. The director's name was Ioshko Gati. But something called "Intersin" wouldn't convert the currency . . .

How nobly lying has evolved over the last twenty years! Girls used to lie that they were engaged to millionaires who owned stud farms. Now they lie about Yugoslav film directors. In the old days a man was proud of his racehorses, while now it's his velvet bedroom slippers from Poland. Gogol's Khlestakov boasted that he was on friendly terms with Pushkin, while my friend Genich came home from Moscow depressed and quiet: he had seen the Kazakh poet Olzhas Suleimanov in the Central Department Store. Even intellectuals lie that they earn a decent salary. I myself always add about twenty rubles to my salary, though what I actually make isn't so bad. Fine . . .

She began to lie. In these situations I always stay quiet. Let them do it. Lying without hope of gain is not lying, it's poetry. I was even sure for some reason that her name wasn't Alla.

Then Klensky showed up.

"Well, that's it," he said. "Three hundred lines in the secretary's folder. Now I can relax."

I took a minute to round off my sketch. I wrote something like this: "Why did the shop-section activists keep silent? Where was the worker's tribunal looking? For it has long been known that greed augmented by impunity ends in crime!"

"Well, let's go," Klensky said. "How long can we wait?"

I turned in the piece and we called up Shablinsky. He reacted sincerely to the invitation. "Rosa is taking an exam. All I've got on me is eight rubles. Tomorrow is a working Wednesday. As they say, it's one thing after another."

We gathered on the staircase landing near the elevator. Zhbankov, one of our photographers, walked by with a camera and flash. Without a word, he took a picture of Alla and withdrew.

"What are our plans?" I asked.

"Let's call Vera."

Vera Khlopina worked in the typing office, although she easily could have become a copyreader or production editor. Nervous, literate and sensible, she was always damaging herself with her hysterical, impertinent tactlessness. The top editors were always happy to attend parties at her apartment. The bachelor atmosphere, two rooms, Vera's girlfriends, music . . . After drinking precisely two glasses of wine, Khlopina would become dangerous. If she didn't like something, she didn't mince words. I remember her once shouting at Weissblat, the deputy director of the youth newspaper, "Just listen to him! He's as black as Louis Armstrong! He couldn't get a job in a garage as a mechanic!"

And women got it from her in the same measure. For everything: for their ability to rationalize their little transgressions, for their imported outfits, for their rich and flabby husbands.

With us three Vera was in sympathy. And rightly so. We weren't careerists, didn't buy cars, didn't puff ourselves up. And we liked Vera. Though our relations with her were strictly comradely. Always blushing, plump, slightly absurd, she was maximally chaste.

It wasn't that Vera liked to drink. It was just that she liked to organize friendly gatherings, to fuss, to run out for Riesling, to prepare hors d'oeuvres. She would say to us, "Right this second I'm going to call Liudka from the haberdashery department. She's incredible! A waist like a wasp's! Huge eyes this size!"

To Liudka she would shout over the phone, "Drop everything! Grab a taxi, and come over here! I'm waiting for you! What? Writers, journalists, all the vodka you can drink, a cake . . ."

As a result, Liudka would show up—tall, slender, with truly huge eyes . . . and a husband who was a captain in the Office of Internal Affairs.

All this was done unselfishly. It was simply that Vera was lonely.

And so we went off to her place. We bought gin and tonic and everything that goes with it. I ought to say that I had come to know what to expect from these evenings. That's because they always progress in the same way. An order has been established once and for all: a kind of concert with all the numbers listed in the program. Shablinsky will tell a story about some fantastic hunt organized by the City Committee. In it there will be woodcocks the size of eagles, a forest hut with a Finnish sauna, Yerevan cognac . . . Then I will interrupt him with my favorite joke: "And among the trees the Regional Party Committee instructors run around dressed in bearskins."

"You're jealous," Shablinsky will say, grinning without malice. "But I did ask you to come."

Then Klensky will tell a story about the harness races at the Hippodrome. And amazing horse names will shoot by in it: Hannibal, Merry Tune, Rock 'n' Roll. "Dukel passes him around the turn, the favorite falls out of step four times. I have six 'express' tickets in my pocket, but at the finish line he breaks into a gallop and he's disqualified!"

Then the hostess will get drunk and tell each of us what she thinks of him. But we're used to it and take no offense. Klensky will get it for his tasteless tie. Me, for my loyalty to some of the higher-ups. Shablinsky for his snobbishness. It will become apparent how exactingly and with what partiality she studies our articles. Then the eternal journalists' conversation begins, over who is ungifted, who is talented, followed by pre-war phonograph records, and then tears, and the miraculously obtained vodka, and the "Do you respect me?" number as a finale. (By the way, that wouldn't be a bad column heading for one of my satirical sketches.)

And basically, that was just how things went. We roasted some kind of little sausages on sticks. Vera got drunk and kissed a portrait of Dobroliubov and said, "What people there used to be!" Then Shablinsky told a vulgar story about Dobroliubov, and I contradicted him without conviction. Alla told some lie, rather touchingly unconvincing, about how Audrey Hepburn had sent her tinting shampoo . . .

After that she went off alone with Mitya to the kitchen. Klensky had a striking method of attracting women. It consisted in talking to them for a long time. What is more, not about himself but about them. And whatever he told them—"You are inclined to trust people, but within certain limits"—his technique never failed to work, whether on student interns from a technical high school or cynical lady journalists from the television studio.

Shablinsky and I quickly began to bore each other. Without even saying goodbye, he left. Vera was asleep. I telephoned Marina, and also set off.

To Alla I had said only one sentence: "If you want, we can disappear quietly." I use this line on everyone. (Women, of course.) Or almost everyone. Just in case. The line has no double meaning and besides, it's harmless.

"That wouldn't be right," Alla had said. "After all, I came to see Mitya."

In the morning there was a lot to do at the office. I was preparing a page about the People's Inspection Unit and nursing myself with mineral water. Shablinsky was busy deciphering his tapes after a conference of educators. Klensky showed up, gloomy and drawn. He talked in an enigmatic and abstract way. "This is the same kind of sham as all the rest of our lives."

At lunchtime the telephone rang. "This is Alla. Have you seen Mitya?"

"Ah," I said. "Hello. How goes it?"

"Hemoglobin two hundred."

"I don't understand."

"What kind of strange question is that, 'How goes it?' Lousy. How else?"

I went to look for Klensky, but they told me he had gone off on an out-of-town assignment. It seems that in the settlement of Kungla a Hero Mother of the Republic had given birth to her eleventh child. I told all this to Alla. She said, "That swine! He didn't say a thing about it . . ."

There was a short silence. I didn't like it. What did I have to do with it? And my page had to be turned in. And it had such an awful title: "The Ballad of a Lost Calculator." And Mitya really was a fine one, going off and not warning the young lady! I began to feel somewhat uncomfortable.

"Would you like," I said, "to have lunch together?"

"Yes, I really should have some lunch. I don't understand my state of mind."

We agreed on where to meet. Then I threw papers all over my desk to make it look as if I was working.

It was a cool and cloudy day in May. Above the glass front of the cafe, linen awnings billowed in the wind. Alla arrived, wearing a huge calico sombrero. She was obviously very proud of it. I looked around me in anguish. All I needed was to be seen in the company of this sombrero by one of Marina's friends. Its brim bumped against the downspouts. Inside the cafe, it turned out that the hat could be easily folded up. We ate some rissoles, then had tea and pastry. Alla behaved as if she could make all sorts of claims on me. I asked: "You're on vacation?"

"Yes," she said, " 'Roman Holidays.' "

"Really, a princess among journalists! How did your mama let you go off by yourself?"

"Why?"

"An unknown city, temptations . . ."

"Two mothers meet, and one says to the other, 'How could you allow your daughter to go off by herself?' And the other mother says, 'Why should I worry? Since she's been nineteen she's been under police supervision.' "

I laughed politely, and called to the waiter. I paid, and we left.

I said, "Well, I am happy to have gazed upon you, Madam."

"*Ciao*, Johnny!" Alla said.

"In that case, not 'Johnny' but 'Giovanni.' "

"*Gud-bi*, Giovanni." And she left in her enormous calico hat, looking like a skinny, capped wood-mushroom.

I hurried back to the office. As it happened, the secretary was already looking for me. At about six that evening the page was ready.

In the evening I went to the theater. They were doing a production called *The Bell*, based on Hemingway. The performance was awful—a combination of *The Magnificent Seven* and *The Young Guard*. In the second act, for example, Robert Jordan shaved himself with a dagger. Incidentally, he was wearing Polish jeans. Just like me.

At the end of the performance, such terrible gunfire began that I walked out without waiting for the ovation. Our city is so good-natured that every theatrical performance ends in wild applause.

I arrived at the office early in the morning. I had an order for a positive review of the play. Numb from tobacco and coffee, I began to write: "Hemingway's works are not effective on stage. This author's single dramatic work had no history in the theater, remaining rather 'a story in dialogue.' 'It reads well,' the author emphasized. The numerous attempts of Hollywood to make screen versions—"

At this moment Vera rang up. I said, "For God's sake, I'm busy! What is it?"

"Come upstairs for a minute."

"What happened?"

"Well, just come up here for a minute!"

"Ah, damn . . ."

Vera was waiting for me on the landing—flushed, nervous, sad.

"You understand, she needs money."

I didn't understand. Rather, I did, but said, "I don't understand."

"Alla needs some money. She doesn't have enough for a plane ticket home."

"Vera, you know me. But till the fourteenth it's out of the question. How much does she need?"

"At least thirty rubles."

"Absolutely out of the question! This month I have no extra pay coming in at all. I owe the bank seventy-five rubles. I'm behind on the payments for my television set. And then, I'm not completely . . . Wait a minute, what about Klensky? After all, she's *his* pal."

"Mitya's gone off somewhere."

"He'll be back soon."

"You have to understand, there will be a catastrophe. Her fiancé called from Saratov . . ."

"From Dvinsk," I said.

"From Saratov. It's not important. He said he'll hang himself if she doesn't come back. Alla's been traveling since February."

"Fine. Let him come and get her."

"He has an exam on Monday."

"That's remarkable," I said. "He may hang himself, but he can't neglect his exam."

"He cried, really cried . . ."

"But look, I don't *have* thirty rubles. And then, it's all so strange somehow, God knows . . . But the main thing is, I don't have the money."

The most interesting part was that I spoke the truth.

"And if you borrowed it from someone?" Vera asked.

"Why should *I* borrow it? She's Klensky's girl. Let him worry about it."

"Maybe we should ask Shablinsky?"

We went to Shablinsky. He even got indignant.

"I had eight rubles. I handed them over like a gentleman. I'd like to put the touch on someone myself. Wait for Mitya, and let him foot the bill for this affair. Listen! I just thought of a good one. You can divide all people into two categories: Bolsheviks or bill-footers."

"Fine," Vera said. "I'll think of something."

And she walked to the door.

"Listen," I said. "If you don't think of something, call me."

"Fine."

"Here's an idea—I'll do an interview with her."

"What use would that be?"

"For the 'Guests of Tallinn' column. A student studies Gothic architecture. Always travels with a volume of Blok. Feeds squirrels in the park. They'll pay her twenty rubles or so, maybe twenty-five."

"Serge, see what you can do!"

"Fine."

At that moment I was called to the editor's office. Henry Franzovich was sitting by the window of his spacious room. The phonograph and television were switched off. The complicated telephone with its white keyboard of buttons lay silent.

"Have a seat," he said. "There's a serious assignment. Moral subjects are poorly represented in our newspaper. You have the widest range of choice. Inveterate alimony evaders, protectionism, government embezzlement . . . I'm counting on you. Go to the People's Court, to the State Automobile Inspection Office . . ."

"I'll think up something."

"Get going," he said. "A moral subject—it's very important."

"O *kay*," I said.

"And remember! The open editorial competition is still on. The best articles will win cash prizes. And the winner will be sent to East Germany."

"Voluntarily?"

"Which is to say?"

"I couldn't even get a visa to go to Bulgaria. I applied last spring."

"You should drink less."

"Fine," I said. "It's not so bad here either."

That day there were still a great many worries, conflicts, arguments, unsettled problems. I attended two conferences, answered four letters, talked on the phone about twenty times, drank cocktails, embraced Marina . . .

A day that went as usual.

And that day in the past—where has it disappeared to? And if it's forgotten, what has moved me six years later to write, "In this story there are no angels or villains, no sinners or saints . . .?"

And what kind of people are we, anyway?

THE FOURTH COMPROMISE

("Evening Tallinn." October 1974.)
ESTONIAN ABC

> On a rainy day by the edge of the woods
> We came upon a huge beast walking.
> "Hello, hello!" we said to him.
> The beast replied politely, "Tereh!"
> And as he spoke a beam of light
> Came out and lit the clouds.

Evening Tallinn is published in Russian. So we invented a new column heading, "Estonian ABC," for juvenile Russian readers. I put the first installments together. Wrote some rather nice verses—about eight of them or so. A universal journalist, I was secretly proud of them.

An instructor from the Central Committee named Vanya Trule called up. "Who wrote this chauvinistic fable?"

"Why chauvinistic?"

"Then it was you who wrote it?"

"Me. What's the matter?"

"A beast figures in it."

"So?"

"He says 'hello' in Estonian. Don't you see the impression that makes? That an Estonian appears to be a beast? Am I a beast? Am I, an instructor of the Central Committee, a beast?"

"Look, this is a fairy tale, a conventional form. An illustration goes with the verses. The little kids meet a bear. The bear has a kind, likeable face. He's a positive character . . ."

"Why does he speak Estonian? Let him speak the language of a capitalist country."

"I don't understand."

"Why do I have to bother explaining this to you! You are obviously not mature enough to write for a Party newspaper. Not mature enough . . ."

An hour later, the chief editor looked in. "The jury is fining you two points."

"Now what? What jury?"

"You forget. The journalists' competition is still going on. Those who write good material will receive prizes. The best of the best will be awarded a trip to the West."

"That's logical. And the worst of the worst—do they get sent to the East?"

"What do you mean by that?"

"Nothing. I was only joking. Is East Germany supposed to be the West?"

"And what is it in your opinion?"

"Well, I would say Japan, *that's* the West!"

"What!" Turonok shouted in fright.

"In the ideological sense," I added.

A shadow of infinite weariness darkened the editor's face. "Dovlatov," he said, "it's impossible to talk with you. Remember, my patience has its limits."

THE FIFTH COMPROMISE

("Soviet Estonia." November 1975)
A MAN HAS BEEN BORN. The annual holiday of Liberation Day is widely observed in the republic. Factories and mills, collective farms, machine-and-tractor stations—all report to the government on the high statistics attained.

And still another milestone has been reached in the last few days. The population of the Estonian capital has reached four hundred thousand. In Tallinn Hospital No. 4, a baby has been born to Maya and Grigori Kuzin—their long-awaited firstborn. It's this little boy who is fated to be the four-hundred-thousandth inhabitant of the city.

"He'll be an athlete," says Chief Doctor Mikel Teppe, smiling.

The happy father awkwardly tries to hide his callused hands. "We'll call our son Lembit," he says. "Let him grow like the folk-hero of that name!"

The famous Tallinn poet Boris Shtein addresses these verses to the happy parents:

> *In factories, in the deepest mines,*
> *On planets strange and far,*
> *I see four hundred thousand heroes,*
> *And your firstborn, too, I see there!*

One remembers the words of Goethe*: "A man is born—an entire world is born!"

I do not know what you will grow up to be, Lembit! A lathe operator or a miner, an officer or a scientist. Only one thing is clear: a man has been born! A man condemned to happiness!

Tallinn is a small city—intimate. You meet a friend on the street and hear, "Hi, I was just looking for you," as though you were in a company cafeteria. The point is, I was surprised to learn just how many people live in Tallinn.

---

* *Author's note:* The fantasy of the author. Goethe did not write this.

THE COMPROMISE

It was like this. Turonok called me in and said, "A constructive idea has turned up. It might make for some effective reporting. Let's discuss the particulars. Just don't get crude with me."

"Why should I be crude? It's useless . . ."

"Actually, you've been crude already," Turonok said, turning gloomy. "You're always being crude, Dovlatov. You're even crude at general meetings. The only time you're not crude is when you're not around for a long time. You think I'm so dull? Think I read nothing but newspapers? You should drop in on me at home sometimes. You should see my library. By the way, I've got some pre-revolutionary editions—"

"Why," I asked, "did you call me in?"

Turonok was silent for a moment. Then he straightened up sharply, as if to change a lyrical pose to a businesslike one. He began to speak with confidence and precision. "Next week is the anniversary of Tallinn's liberation. The day will be widely observed everywhere, including the pages of this newspaper. We'll cover all its various aspects—economic, cultural, human-interest . . . Every department is working something up. There's a job for you, too. To be specific: According to the data issued by the Bureau of Statistics, the city has around four hundred thousand inhabitants. This figure is somewhat relative, just as the city limits are. So here's what it comes down to. We talked it over and decided: the four-hundred-thousandth inhabitant of Tallinn is about to be born on the eve of the jubilee."

"There's something here I don't quite understand."

"Go to the maternity hospital. Wait for the first newborn. Get the measurements. Interview the happy parents, the doctor who delivered the baby. Naturally, get photographs. The story will run in the jubilee issue. The pay—I know this is not without significance to you—is double."

"You should have said so in the first place."

"Mercantilism is one of your more unpleasant traits," Turonok said.

"Debts," I said. "Alimony."

"You drink a lot."

"It happens."

"Let's cut this short. The general idea is, a happy man has just been born. I'd even put it this way—a man condemned to happiness!" This foolish phrase pleased the editor so much that he repeated it twice. "A man condemned to happiness! In my opinion, not bad. Maybe we'll use it as a headline: 'A MAN CONDEMNED TO HAPPINESS.'"

"We'll see," I said.

"And remember"—Turonok stood up, closing our conversation—"the infant has to be publicizable."

"Which means?"

"Which means meeting all requirements. No damaged goods, nothing gloomy. No cesarean sections. No unwed mothers. A complete set of parents. A healthy boy meeting all the social requirements."

"It has to be a boy?"

"Yes, a boy is somehow more symbolic."

"Henry Franzovich, about those photographs. If you think about it, newborns can look pretty awful."

"Choose the best one. You can wait. There's time."

"We'd have to wait at least four months. Any earlier, it will hardly look human. Some people still don't after fifty years."

"Listen," said Turonok, turning angry, "don't give me that demagoguery! You have an assignment. The material has to be ready by Wednesday. You're a professional journalist. Why are we wasting time?"

He's right, I thought. Why indeed?

I went down to the bar and ordered a gin and a sandwich. I noticed Zhbankov, the photographer, not very sober, and I waved to him. He sat down next to me with a wineglass of vodka and broke off half of my sandwich.

"You should go home," I said. "The office is full of bosses."

Zhbankov emptied the wineglass and said, "You know, I've already made a mess of things. Did you see the shot I took for Fedya's piece?"

"I don't read newspapers."

"Fedya had a piece in *Youth*. More exactly, a sketch. 'Three Against the Storm.' About divers. How they search, you know, for valuable sunken cargo. With a storm moving in, no less. So that was my photograph. Two big guys sitting on a log. And a hose sticking up out of the water—that's one of their buddies keeping busy on the bottom. So naturally I go out and shoot it, tie up the rowboat, and forget the whole thing. But then, as I walk through the port, I hear laughing. What's going on, you know? It turns out to be quite a story. It seems there's a fellow down there named Mironenko, chief of the auxiliary shop. Earlier that day he happens to walk out of the lunchroom and light up a cigarette by the third mooring. Et cetera, et cetera. Throws away the cigarette. Gets ready to spit, pardon the expression. And spits out his teeth. His false ones, naturally. And he's got about eight hundred rubles' worth of gold in them. So he runs to the divers. 'Comrades, help!' And they yell back, 'We'll get them after work.' 'I'll make it worth your while.' 'Stand us a bottle each?' 'What a question!' So they finish work and start diving around. And now Fedya comes by from another assignment. Takes in the scene. 'What are you doing there?' he says. Makes himself important, you know. And the divers get a little shy. 'Your mother, such-and-such,' they answer, 'some valuable cargo has sunk.' And Fedya asks like an idiot, 'What's your name? What's your name?' And these guys give him all the right answers. 'What do you like to do in your rare moments of leisure?' 'Music,' they say, 'painting . . .' 'And why are you working so late?' 'A storm is coming in, we're in a hurry,' they say. Fedya calls me at the newspaper. I show up and shoot some pictures without asking around. The main thing was, it was some kind of manmade harbor. No storm could ever get there."

"You should go home," I said.

"Wait, the main thing wasn't even that. Later I found out how the whole business ended. The divers did find the guy's dentures. Mironenko was in bliss up to his eyebrows. So he herds them all to a tavern. Orders vodka. Has a few shots. Starts to demonstrate his dentures to everybody. 'I want to thank these kids,' he says, 'who saved my life and found them. Eagles,' he says, 'heroes of labor, Stakhanovites.' Shows them his dentures at one table, then another. The doorman comes up to take a look, the trombonist from the band. The waitresses shake their heads in amazement. And Mironenko opens the sixth bottle with the divers. Suddenly he does a double take—no dentures. Somebody took them. He yells, 'Give them back, you bastards!' Fat chance. Now even the divers can't help."

"Fine," I said. "I've got to go."

I didn't feel like going to the maternity ward. I find the atmosphere in hospitals depressing. The rubber plants get me down.

I dropped by the office to see Marina. She said, "Oh, it's you. Sorry, I'm busy."

"Has something happened?"

"What could happen? There's a lot of work."

"What kind of work?"

"The jubilee and all that. After all, we're dull people. We don't write novels."

"Why are you in such a bad mood?"

"And why should I be in a good mood? You're always disappearing somewhere. One moment you're madly in love, then you're gone for a week, playing around."

"What do you mean, 'playing around'? I was on assignment near Saaremaa. I'm all bitten up from the bedbugs in the hotel."

"Those aren't bedbug bites," Marina said, squinting suspiciously. "Those are from some woman. Some revolting little tart. What do they see in you, I wonder. Never any money, always with a hangover . . . I'm amazed you haven't caught some infection already."

"What can you catch from a bedbug?"

"If only you'd stop lying! Who was that tall, fidgety redhead? I saw you from the bus this morning."

"That was no fidgety redhead. That was the metaphysical poet Vladimir Erle. He's letting his hair grow."

Suddenly I realized that she was about to burst into tears. Marina always wept despondently, bitterly, with little yelps, holding nothing back—like an actress after a performance.

"I beg you, calm down. Everything will be all right. Everyone knows how attached I am to you."

Marina got out a tiny rose-colored handkerchief and wiped her eyes. She began to speak more calmly. "Can you be serious for a moment?"

"Of course."

"I'm not so sure. You're completely irresponsible, like a skylark. You have no address, or possessions, or ambitions. You have no deep attachments. I'm just a random stopping point in space. But I'm already pushing forty. I have to put my life in some kind of order."

"I'm also pushing forty. More exactly, I'm over thirty. And I don't know what that means, 'to put your life in order.' You want to get married? But what will that change? What will that idiotic stamp give us? It's a horse-brand. While things are good, I'm here. When I get tired of them, I'll go. That's the way it will always be."

"I don't plan to get married. Anyway, what kind of husband would you make! It's just that I want to have a child. Otherwise it will be too late."

"So have a child. But think of what's in store for him."

"You always paint things in such dark colors. Millions of people live and work honestly. Anyway, how can I have a child alone?"

"Why alone? I'll . . . participate. And as for the material side of the question, you earn three times as much as I do. Which means, practically speaking, you don't need me to support you."

"I was talking about something else."

The telephone rang. Marina picked it up. "Yes? . . . Well, that's great. He's right here."

I waved my hands no.

Marina nodded understandingly. "I mean, he just left. . . . No, I have no idea. He's probably off drinking somewhere."

Well, I thought, the little bitch.

"Stekhanovsky is looking for you. He wants to pay you back some money you loaned him."

"What's wrong with him?"

"He got paid for his book."

"*A Caravan to the Skies*?"

"Why '*Caravan*'? The book is called *To Be Continued*."

"It's the same thing," I said. "Fine. I've got to go."

"Where are you off to? If it's no secret."

"Picture this—the maternity hospital."

I glanced at the tables heaped with newspapers, caught a smell of cigarette smoke and glue, and felt such a strong pang of boredom and bitterness that even the hospital didn't seem so bad.

Outside the door I realized that Marina had shouted out, "Well, get lost, you pitiful drunk!"

I got on a bus and headed for Karl Marx Street. In the bus, I fell asleep unexpectedly and woke up, after a minute, with a headache. Crossing the hall of the maternity hospital, I caught a glimpse of myself in the mirror and turned away.

A woman in a white smock came toward me. "Unauthorized visitors are not permitted."

"How about authorized authors?" I asked.

The nurse froze in confusion. I held out my press pass and climbed to the second floor. A few women in shapeless white coats were smoking on the landing.

"Where can I find the doctor?"

"One flight up, across from the elevator."

Across from the elevator means that the doctor is a modest man. Across from the elevator it must be noisy—doors slamming.

I walked in. An Estonian of about sixty was standing in front of an open window doing exercises.

I can spot an Estonian right away, and I'm never wrong. Nothing raucous or flamboyant about them. Invariably, the tie and the crease in the pants. A rather poor line to the chin and a calm look in the eyes. Anyway, what Russian does exercises alone?

I held out my ID.

"Dr. Mikel Teppe. Please have a seat. How can I be of help?"

I told him what I was there for. The doctor was not surprised. In general, no matter what the press comes up with, it's hard to surprise the average reader. He's used to everything.

"I don't think it should be difficult," Teppe said. "The clinic is enormous."

"Are you notified about every birth?"

"It can be arranged." He picked up the receiver, said something in Estonian, then turned to me. "Are you interested in the actual labor?"

"God forbid! All I want to do is write up the data, take a look at the baby, and talk with the father."

The doctor made another call and once again said something in Estonian. Then he said to me, "There's a woman in labor right now. I'll check again in a few minutes. I'm sure everything will be all right. The mother is such a big, healthy blonde." The doctor was getting carried away.

"And you yourself," I asked, "are you married?"

"Of course."

"Do you have any children?"

"One son."

"Do you ever wonder what's in store for him?"

"Why should I wonder? I know exactly what's in store for him. He's in for a strict-regime labor camp. I consulted a lawyer. They've already got from him a written promise that he won't leave town, which means they must be about to arrest him." Teppe spoke calmly and simply, as though we were talking about the most natural thing in the world.

I lowered my voice and asked in a confidential tone, "The Soldatov case?"

"What?" the doctor said, not understanding.

"Your son—did he take part in the Estonian Spring?"

"My son," Teppe said distinctly, "is a black marketeer and a drunk. And I can only stop worrying about him somewhat when he's locked up."

We were both silent.

"At one time I worked as a medic on the islands. Then I served in the Estonian Army Corps. I was given a high position. I don't know what we did wrong. His mother and I are people with a positive outlook, while our son has a negative one."

"I wouldn't mind hearing his side of the story."

"It's impossible to listen to him. I say to him, 'Yura, why do you despise me? I've obtained everything I have through hard work. I haven't had an easy life. Now I have a high position. Why do you think they made me—a humble medic—a chief physician?' And he says, 'Because all your smart colleagues were shot.' As if I shot them."

THE COMPROMISE

The telephone rang.

"Speaking," Teppe said. "Excellent." Then he changed to Estonian. The conversation was about centimeters and kilograms.

"There we are," he told me. "A birth in the ninth ward. Four kilos two hundred grams and fifty-eight centimeters. Want to see it?"

"No, thanks. Babies all look the same."

"The mother's last name is Okas. Khilia Okas. Born 1946. Works as a regulator in the Punane Factory. The father's is Magabcha."

"What does that mean—'Magabcha'?"

"That's his last name. He's from Ethiopia. He's studying at the Merchant Marine Academy."

"Black?"

"More like chocolate."

"Listen," I said, "this is interesting. We could play up internationalism. The friendship of nations. Are they married?"

"Of course. He writes her notes every day and signs them, 'Your carob bar.'"

"Can I use your telephone?"

"Help yourself."

I called the office. Turonok came to the phone.

"Yes? Turonok speaking."

"Henry Franzovich, a little boy has just been born."

"What? Who is this?"

"It's Dovlatov. From the maternity hospital. You gave me an assignment."

"Oh, yes. I remember."

"Well, a little boy has been born. Big, healthy. Fifty-eight centimeters. Four kilos two hundred grams. The father is Ethiopian . . ."

An uneasy silence.

"I don't understand," Turonok said.

"An Ethiopian. He comes from Ethiopia. He's a student here," I said. "A Marxist," I added for some reason.

"Are you drunk?" Turonok asked sharply.

"How can you say that? I'm on assignment."

"On assignment. When did that ever stop you? Who vomited all over the Regional Party Headquarters last December?"

"Henry Franzovich, I can't tie up the line for long. A little boy has just been born. His father belongs to a friendly nation."

"You mean to say he's black?"

"More like chocolate."

"That is, a Negro?"

"Naturally."

"What is there natural about this?"

"Isn't an Ethiopian a human being?"

"Dovlatov," Turonok said, in a voice choked with torment, "Dovlatov, I'll fire you . . . for attempting to discredit the very best . . . Leave me in peace with your rotten Ethiopian! Wait for a normal—do you hear me?—*normal* human baby!"

"Fine," I said. "I was only asking."

The line went dead. Teppe looked at me with sympathy.

"It won't work," I told him.

"I had doubts right away, but I didn't want to say anything."

"Well, fine."

"Would you like some coffee?" He took a brown jar out of a cabinet. The telephone rang again. Teppe talked for a long time in Estonian. Obviously it had nothing to do with me.

I waited till he finished and then unexpectedly heard myself ask, "Could I use your cot to take a nap?"

"Of course," Teppe said without surprise. "Would you like to put my raincoat over you?"

"This is all right."

Behind a screen I took off my shoes and stretched out on

the cot. I had to concentrate. Otherwise the contours of reality might become hopelessly lost. Suddenly I saw myself from the outside, distracted and absurd. Who am I? What am I doing here? Why am I lying behind a screen waiting for God knows what? And how stupidly my life is going.

When I woke up, Teppe was standing over me.

"Excuse me, I'm sorry if I startled you, but a lady you know has just given birth."

Marina, I thought with a light flash of terror. (As everyone knows, fear can be felt in even slight degrees.) Then, pushing this crazy thought aside, I asked, "What do you mean, 'a lady I know'?"

"A journalist from *Youth* magazine. Rumiantseva."

"Ah, Lena, the wife of Borya Shtein. Of course. That's why I haven't seen her since May."

"She gave birth five minutes ago."

"This has possibilities. The editor will be happy. The father is a famous Tallinn poet. The mother is a journalist. Both are in the Party. Shtein will undoubtedly write a ballad for the occasion."

"Very glad for you."

I called Shtein. "Greetings," I said. "You're to be congratulated."

"It's still early for that. I get the answer on Wednesday."

"What answer?"

"About whether I'm going to Sweden or not. They tell me I have no experience traveling in capitalist countries. But how can I get experience if they won't let me out? Have you been to any capitalist countries?"

"No. I couldn't even get permission to go to a socialist country. I applied to go to Bulgaria."

"But I've even been to Yugoslavia. Yugoslavia is practically capitalist."

"I'm calling from the clinic. Your son has just been born."

"Your mother!" Shtein shouted. "Your mother!"

Teppe handed me a scribbled sheet.

"Height," I said, "fifty-six, weight three kilos nine hundred grams. Lena feels fine."

"Your mother!" Shtein could not stop. "I'll be right there. I'll take a taxi."

Now I had to call the photographer.

"Call him, call him," Teppe said.

I called Zhbankov. His wife answered.

"Mikhail Vladimirovich is not well," she said.

"What—drunk?" I asked.

"Like a pig. Was it you who got him drunk?"

"Nothing of the sort. Anyway, I'm at work."

"Well, sorry."

I called Malkiel. "Come over and take a picture of a baby for the jubilee issue. Shtein has a new son. The pay is double, by the way."

"You want to write about that baby?"

"Why not?"

"Why not? Because Shtein is a Jew. And every Jew has to be submitted for approval. You're fantastically naïve, Serge."

"I wrote about Kaplan and didn't submit him for approval."

"Tell me more. Tell me how you wrote about Gliksman. Kaplan is a member of the Regional Party Bureau. He's been written up hundreds of times. Don't start comparing Kaplan with Shtein."

"I'm not comparing them. Shtein is much nicer."

"So much the worse for him."

"I get the point. Thanks for warning me."

I said to Teppe, "It seems that Shtein won't work, either."

"I had my doubts."

"Then who woke me up?" I asked.

"I woke you up. But I had doubts."

"So now what?"

"Very soon another woman will finish labor. She might have given birth already. I'll call right now."

"I'll just take a little walk outside."

Cats were prowling around the dreary hospital courtyard. The leafless poplars made harsh scraping sounds. A skinny, slouching boy in his teens passed by, rolling a serving cart with a coffee urn on it. His faded blue attendant's smock made him look like an old woman.

Shtein appeared from around the corner.

"Ah, congratulations," I said.

"Thanks, old man, thanks. I just dropped off a basket of food for Lenka. I'm in a fantastic mood. We should have a drink to celebrate."

Some drinking one can do with you, I thought. It has to end badly.

I didn't want to disappoint him. I didn't want to tell him that his baby was a reject. But Shtein already knew that something was up.

"You're writing an article about the jubilee?"

"I'm trying to."

"And you want to make my family famous?"

"The trouble is," I said, "we need a worker-peasant family. And you're intellectuals."

"Too bad. I already wrote some lines in the taxi. Here's how the poem ends:

> *In factories, in the deepest mines,*
> *On planets strange and far,*
> *I see four hundred thousand heroes,*
> *And my firstborn, too, I see there!"*

I said, "Why firstborn? You have a grown daughter."

"From my first marriage."

"Ah," I said, "then that's all right."

Shtein thought for a while and suddenly said, "This means that anti-Semitism really does exist, doesn't it?"

"Looks like it."

"How could it appear in our country? Here, in a country where it seems—"

I interrupted him. "In a country where the 'founding corpse' has still not been buried. A country whose very name is a lie."

"You think everything is a lie!"

"There are lies in my journalism and in your lousy poems! When did you ever see an Estonian in space?"

"That was a metaphor."

"A metaphor. There are dozens of euphemisms like that for lies."

"So you're the only honest man left. And who wrote that long article about the Baikal-Amur Main Line? Who praised that old police agent Timofeyev?"

"I'm quitting this business. You'll see, I'll quit."

"Wait until then to criticize anyone else."

"Don't be angry."

"You've spoiled my mood. I'll see you."

Teppe met me at the door.

"Kuzina in the sixth ward has just given birth. Here's the information. She herself is Estonian, a trolley-car driver. Her husband is a turner in a shipyard, Russian, Party member. The child is within all bounds of the norm."

"Thank God. I think this will work. I'd better call in just to make sure."

Turonok said, "Now, that's excellent. Arrange for the child to be called Lembit."

THE COMPROMISE

"Henry Franzovich," I begged, "who would call their child Lembit? It's so old-fashioned, you only see it in folklore—"

"Let them call it Lembit. What's the difference to them? Lembit has a good, manly, symbolic ring to it. In the jubilee issue it will catch everyone's eye."

"Could you call your own child Bova? Or Mikula?"

"Don't give me any of your demagoguery. You have an assignment. The material has to be ready by Wednesday. If they refuse to call it Lembit, promise them some money."

"How much?"

"Twenty-five rubles or so. I'll send a photographer. What's the newborn's last name?"

"Kuzin. Sixth ward."

"Lembit Kuzin. Sounds beautiful. Now get on with it."

I asked Teppe, "How can I find the father?"

"There he is. He's sitting down there on the lawn."

I went downstairs.

"Hello," I said, "are you Kuzin?"

"I'm Kuzin, all right," he said, "but what good is it?"

Evidently Comrade Kuzin was in a philosophic mood.

"Allow me to congratulate you," I said. "Your baby turns out to be the four-hundred-thousandth inhabitant of our city. I am from the newspaper. I would like to write about your family."

"What is there to write about?"

"Well, about your life."

"What about it? We don't live badly. We work, like everyone else. We broaden our horizons. We use our leadership abilities."

"We should go somewhere to talk."

"You mean, have a drink?" Kuzin brightened. He was a tall man with a granite chin and childlike, innocent eyelashes. He got up from the lawn energetically and brushed off his knees.

We headed for the Kosmos, and found a table by the window. The hall was still uncrowded.

"I've got eight rubles on me," Kuzin said, "plus a bottle of poison." He pulled a bottle of Cuban rum out of his briefcase and hid it behind the curtain. "Shall we start with three hundred grams apiece?"

"And beer," I said, "if it's cold."

We ordered three hundred grams of vodka, two salads, and a chopped-meat cutlet each.

"Would you care for a plate of smoked fish?" asked the waiter.

"Relax!" Kuzin said to him.

The hall was deserted. On a raised platform four musicians had taken their places—piano, guitar, bass, and drums. The oak music stands were decorated with tin lyres.

The guitarist furtively wiped his shoes with a handkerchief. Then he walked to the microphone and announced, "By the request of our friends, who have just returned from the resort town of Vasalemma . . ."

A significant pause.

". . . we will now play the lyrical song 'Raindrops Are Falling on My Kisser.'"

An unimaginable din began, heightened by the amplifier. The musicians shouted something unintelligible in chorus.

"Do you know what Vasalemma is?" Kuzin asked, amused. "It's the biggest prison-camp town in Estonia. Maximum-security prisons, transit stations, strict-regime camps . . . Well, let's have one!" He raised his glass.

"To you! To your son!"

"To our meeting! That it may not be our last!"

Two couples danced, aloof, between tables. The hall was filling up. More and more waiters in black-and-white outfits appeared, carrying trays of glasses and carafes and plates of food.

"Another round?"

We drank again.

Kuzin took a few quick bites of food and began to talk. "The way things went with us—it's pure theater. I was working at the shipyard, living alone. Well, I met this woman, also alone. Not exactly bad-looking, and quiet. She started coming by, doing the laundry, ironing—that sort of thing. We got together around Easter. No, I'm wrong—around Ascension Day. Before that, what did I have after work? A vacuum. How much can you stuff yourself? We lived together about a year. How she happened to get pregnant I don't know. She used to lie there like a codfish. I'd say, 'You can't fall asleep?' And she'd say, 'No, I can hear everything.' 'Not much heat in you,' I'd say. And she'd say, 'There must be a light on in the kitchen.' 'Where'd you get that idea?' 'Listen how the meter's clicking.' 'You could take some lessons from it.' That's how we lived for a year."

Kuzin reached behind the curtain for the bottle of rum and tilted it invitingly. We drank again.

The guitarist straightened his jacket and shouted, "By the request of Tolya B., sitting by the door, we will now sing . . ."

A pause, while the volume became greater.

". . . we will now sing the lyrical song 'What's the Poison You Gave Me to Drink?' "

"Are you married yourself?" Kuzin asked with interest.

"I was."

"And now?"

"Now, it seems, no."

"Do you have any children?"

"Yes."

"Many?"

"Many. A daughter."

"Maybe you'll have some more?"

"I doubt it."

"Too bad for the kids. The kids aren't to blame. I call them Flowers of Life. Shall we have another?"

"I'm all for it."

"With beer."

"Naturally."

I knew that three more glasses and it would all be over. It's nice to drink early in the day with this thought in mind: Once you're drunk, the whole day is free.

"Listen," I said, "call your son Lembit."

"Why Lembit?" Kuzin was surprised. "We wanted Volodya. What on earth is that—Lembit?"

"Lembit is a name."

"What is Volodya—not a name?"

"Lembit is from folklore."

"What's that—folklore?"

"The art of the people."

"What does the art of the people have to do with it? My own private son I want to call Volodya. What he'll be called later is another problem. For example, I was named Grisha, and what happened? Who did I grow up to be? Guzzler. That's what they should have called me in the first place. Bottoms up."

We now drank without bothering to eat anything.

"We could call him Volodya," Kuzin proposed, "and get God knows what. Of course, much depends on upbringing—"

"Listen," I said, "call him Lembit temporarily. Our editor has promised to lay out some dough, and then next month you can change the name when you register him."

"How much?" Kuzin was interested.

"Twenty-five rubles."

"That's two half bottles and some snacks. In a bar, of course."

"At least. Wait here, I'll call."

I went downstairs, found a pay telephone, and called the office. The editor happened to be right there.

"Henry Franzovich! Everything is O *kay*! The papa is Russian, the mother is Estonian. Both work at a shipyard."

"Your voice sounds funny," Turonok said.

"It's the pay phone. Henry Franzovich, send Hubert over right away with the money."

"What money? What are you talking about?"

"The bait. So they'll name the baby Lembit. The father has agreed to twenty-five rubles. Otherwise he says he'll call it Adolf."

"Dovlatov, you're drunk!" Turonok said.

"Nothing of the kind."

"All right, let's settle it. The material has to be ready by Wednesday. Hubert will leave in five minutes. Wait for him at Town Hall Square. He'll give you the key."

"The key?"

"Yes. The symbolic key. The key of happiness. Present it to the father with the proper ceremony. The key cost three-eighty. I'm deducting it from the twenty-five rubles."

"That's dishonest," I said.

The editor hung up.

I went back upstairs. Kuzin was napping, his head on the tablecloth. Under his cheek a bread dish stuck up sideways.

I shook Kuzin by the shoulder.

"Allo," I said, "wake up! Hubert's waiting for us."

"What?" he said, startled. "Hubert? You said Lembit."

"Lembit is something else. Lembit is your son. Temporarily."

"Yes, I've had a son."

"His name is Lembit."

"First Lembit, then Volodya."

"And Hubert is bringing us the money."

"I've got money," Kuzin said. "Eight rubles."

"We have to pay. Where's the waiter?"

"Allo! Smoked fish, where are you?" Kuzin yelled.

The waiter appeared with a dreary expression on his face. "One plate has been broken," he announced.

"Aha!" said Kuzin. "That was me hitting my head on the table—bang!" Sheepishly he took some bits of broken crockery out of his jacket pocket.

"And one toilet stall is a mess," the waiter added. "You should have aimed more carefully."

"Get the hell out of here!" Kuzin shouted suddenly. "Do you hear? Or I'll polish your bald spot!"

"I don't advise you to try it while I'm carrying out my duties. You might find yourself in jail."

I slipped some money into his hand. "Pardon us," I said. "My friend here has just had a son. He's a little upset."

"If you have to drink so much, at least conduct yourselves decently," the waiter said, backing off.

We paid and walked out. It was raining. Hubert's car was parked near the Town Hall. He signaled and opened the door. We climbed in.

"Here's the money," Hubert said. "The boss is worried that you might start drinking."

I took some bills and change from him in the dark.

Hubert held out a heavy box.

"And what is this?"

"Something he picked up in Pskov."

I opened the box. Inside was an electroplated key the size of a small balalaika.

"Ah," I said, "the key of happiness!"

I opened the door and threw the key into a trash can. Then I said to Hubert, "Let's go have a drink."

"I'm driving."

"Leave the car and we'll all go."

"I have to take the boss home."

"He can get home himself, the fat slob."

"Look, they promised me an apartment. If it weren't for that—"

"Live with me," Kuzin said, "and I'll send my woman to the country. To Usokhi, near Pskov. They haven't seen margarine there since summer."

"I've got to go," Hubert said.

We went out into the rain again. The windows of the Astoria Restaurant shone invitingly. A street lamp picked out from the darkness a multicolored puddle by the door.

Is it worth going into what happened next? How my companion climbed onto the stage and yelled, "They've sold out Russia"? And hit the doorman so hard that his cap rolled into the closet? And how we were taken to the police station? And how they let us go, thanks to my press pass? And how I lost my note pad with all my notes? And how I then lost Kuzin himself?

I woke up in Marina's room in the middle of the night. A pale light filled the room. The ticking of the alarm clock was unbearably loud. I smelled ammonia and damp clothes.

I touched a swelling scratch on my temple.

Marina sat next to me, sad and a little drawn. She was stroking my hair softly. She kept stroking and saying, "Poor boy . . . poor boy . . . poor boy . . ."

Who's she talking to, I thought. Who's she talking to?

THE SIXTH COMPROMISE

("Evening Tallinn." Weekly radio broadcast schedule. March 1976.) . . . 13.30.
"A MEETING WITH AN INTERESTING PERSON. Ilya Merkin. The economy of the future."
  The focus of this week's radio-essay by L. Agapova and S. Dovlatov will be Ilya Merkin, Doctor of Economic Sciences. You will hear his lively and exciting account of economic progress in the USSR and the irreversible financial crisis in the present-day West. During intermission there will be a news broadcast and a musical entr'acte.

Four years later, a deep scar was to appear on the face of journalist Lida Agapova, the result of being struck with a metal T-square. A self-taught architect named Degtiarenko, who was supposed to be the subject of a social-affairs broadcast that was finally never aired, had rushed at her with a mad howl. Six weeks before this disgraceful scene the journalist had first learned about the *Mobile kooperato* project and its brilliant creator, who worked as an unskilled laborer in one of Tallinn's factories. She then wrote a script about Degtiarenko for the weekly interview series "A Meeting with an Interesting Person." The radio station's technical department asked for blueprints. An expert named Chubarov examined them. He held the two soiled and quivering pieces of tracing paper in his well-groomed hands and said, "Original! Highly original!"

With relief and pride the journalist exclaimed, "And he's only had four years of schooling!"

"And what about you?" the expert said peevishly. "Do you know what this is?"

"*Mobile kooperato*. A mobile home. The dwelling of the future."

"This is a trailer," Chubarov interrupted. "An ordinary trailer. And your Le Corbusier should be hospitalized at once."

The broadcast was condemned there and then. His hopes shattered, Degtiarenko hit Lida over the head with a metal T-square. The career of Lida Agapova, freelance contributor to the Tallinn radio station, was interrupted for a long time. All of this happened four years after the time of the present story. In the present story she is on her way to the tramcar stop.

It had been an overcast morning; earlier, a sub-freezing night. A sleepy pigeon had wandered along the eaves, scratching at the tin plate. Then the alarm clock, chilly slippers, the communal scramble to use the toilet; tea, warped slices of moist cheese, the hum of the electric shaver—her husband hurrying to get to work. Her daughter: "I *asked* you not to touch my bathrobe!" And at last the coolness of the indifferent streets, wind, zinc-colored puddles, miniature dogs in the square, the grind of the approaching tram.

I'll try to describe her, though Agapova's appearance has no special significance.

Imported rubber boots. A heavy brown skirt that doesn't accentuate her steps. A zippered synthetic jacket that makes a rustling sound. The blue-crested uniform cap of the Tallinn Polytechnic. A determined face that always looks pinched by the cold. No trace of cosmetics. A missing tooth in the corner of her smile. Only the eyes express astonishment; the eyebrows are as motionless as the ribbon of a finish-line.

She reaches the tram stop.

"Look how well dressed girls are these days! That smart little coat over there—that's imported, not ours. Instead of buttons, some kind of pine cones. But nice to look at . . . Or look at that girl in the professional uniform. Cornflowers on her behind, and the proud way she walks, as if she were Lollobrigida. Once in the summertime I saw a girl walking barefoot. Not drunk either, just purposely barefoot. In the middle of the city. Walking, showing off. Actually, my clothes are all imported too, only from the People's Democracies. So nobody looks at them twice. But where do they get theirs from? Do they hang around with foreigners? Shameful! But nice to look at . . ."

Straining, the doors of the tramcar slide apart. A short, agonizing assault. A broad army back blocks her way, her cheek pushed up against nappy, suffocating cloth. She grabs onto the handrail. Life around her reflects back, miniaturized, off the nickel-plated tube.

"Wait, don't drop that kopeck in the farebox. I'll take it as my change."

Lida tries to catch her balance over the metal farebox.

"Go on, move yourself! She stands there like a dummy."

The main thing is not to get annoyed, to take things with a sense of humor. Rush hour, a typical occurrence. Now what's important is to locate a source of positive emotions. Look, someone's giving a seat to that old grandma. A student is studying an abstract. Even that soldier has a decent face.

And once again—the street, cars, people, the pleasing and exciting neutrality of people and cars. Then the vestibule, a broad marble staircase, its carpeted runner threadbare on the curve of each step. A sign: "Propaganda Department."

Lida knocks and enters. Everyone is terribly glad to see her. Kuleshov comes out with his usual banalities. Verochka Kotova smiles without lifting her eyes. Zhenia Turin helps her off with her coat. Moralevich asks, "Did you hear about last Thursday? Yurna himself is pleased with you."

"Really!"

Even Valeri Chmutov, the chronic failure, joins in the smoking. Chmutov was an actor. He possessed an inborn gift, a beautiful low voice of an astonishing timbre. He had worked as an announcer. Six months earlier, his career had undergone a tragic reversal. He had the job of starting off an early morning broadcast which went on the air live. All he had to do was say a few words: "Dear Radio Listeners! Your weekly program, 'Greetings Comrade!' is on the air." That was it. From then on, it was all music and tapes. Chmutov would collect his eleven rubles.

Chmutov had gone into the glass broadcast booth. Sat down. Pulled over the microphone. Repeated the text to himself. Turned over his cuffs so that the cufflinks wouldn't tap on the table. Waited for the "on the air" bulb to light up. His mood, after the previous day's drinking spree, was low. The bulb did not light up.

"Dear Radio Listeners," Chmutov said pensively.

It was hard for him to move his tongue, which felt scorched by all the cheap port he had drunk. The bulb did not light up.

"Dear Radio Listeners," Chmutov repeated again. "Oh God, how revolting . . . Dear Radio Listeners . . . Yes, that was a mistake, getting so drunk last night . . ."

The bulb did not light up. As it happened, it had burned out. This happens once in a hundred years.

"This is your weekly program, coming to you live," Chmutov rehearsed. "Oh, what the hell! That's it. I've had it."

Behind the glass the contorted face of the producer suddenly appeared. Chmutov froze. The door was flung open. The struggling announcer was thrown down the stairs. His hungover incantations could be heard on all the airwaves. He was fired. But the story doesn't end there.

Chmutov went off to Pskov and found a job as a program director. The local broadcast took about an hour and a half. The rest of the time was filled by Moscow and Leningrad. Chmutov was in a state of bliss. Everyone regarded him as the master from the capital.

One day he was doing a broadcast. Suddenly the door

squeaked, and a big brown dog walked in. (Whose was it? Where had it come from?) Cautiously, Chmutov patted it. The dog flattened its ears and shut its eyes tight. Its nose shone like a tiny boxer's glove.

"The country workers send in this report—" Chmutov read.

And just at that moment the dog suddenly began to bark. Perhaps out of pleasure. No one, apparently, had ever spoiled it with kindness.

Chmutov was fired again, only this time for good and from everywhere. When he told people about the dog, no one believed him. They were sure he had done the barking himself in the middle of a hangover.

Chmutov left for Tallinn. He would sit around the radio station for days, waiting for his break.

Everyone avoids failures. Lida always smiled at him.

She had worked for the Propaganda Department for a long time. Everyone liked her. On this day the department head, Nina Ignatyevna, gave her an especially friendly nod. "Lidochka, come to my office."

In her office: silence, a polished table, innumerable ball-point pens. Behind the glass doors of the bookcase glittered travel mementoes and encyclopedia spines. In Nina Ignatyevna's drawer you could find lipstick, a little mirror, and eyeshadow. And it's always pleasant to see an attractive young woman in such an important office.

"Lidochka, I want to give you a new series to write for, a program we'll call 'A Meeting with an Interesting Person.' Your subjects don't necessarily have to be scientists or astronauts. The range of choice is exceptionally wide. Someone with an admirable hobby, or a sudden fad, or a certain thread in his life story. Let's say there's an unassuming, well-established chief accountant who secretly . . . I don't know, whatever you come up with. Nothing comes to mind at the moment. Let's say he secretly—"

"Abuses little children," Lida prompted.

"I had something else in mind. Let's say he secretly—"
"Studies Sanskrit."
"Something on that order. Only more significant socially. Let's say a policeman helps someone track down his own close friend or relative . . ."
"There was a film like that."
"I can't give you anything concrete. You'll have to think about it. Here, for example. At the Kalev Factory they shot a film called *A Woman Alone*. You remember, starring Doronina. Well, it turns out that a kid who took part in the shooting has become the head of one of the shop sections."
"I like that theme," Lida said. "I feel it."
"The theme has already been used by Arvid Kiisk. As I was saying, something on that order. You'll have to think up something on your own. Suppose an old general goes into a hospital for an operation. And realizes that his surgeon was his former orderly."
"What's his name?" Lida asked.
"Whose?"
"What's the name of that general? Or his orderly?"
"I'm speaking hypothetically. Whatever theme, the main thing should be the unexpected—mystery, chance. A life with many levels. Outside one thing, inside another."
"That's how it is for most people," Lida sighed.
"In brief, get on with it," Nina Ignatyevna said, with the barest annoyance.
Lida left her office.
She had grown up among interesting people since childhood. Her father had known Ehrenburg. The drawing teacher at school was said to have been an unrecognized genius. Later she had been courted by a bohemian who had even written verses. The professors at her institute were remarkable for their eccentricities, one for always having his fly open. Her husband was an

interesting man, a senior economist who still made grammatical mistakes in his writing. Her daughter was a very mysterious person—she hardly ever said anything, and lately had been so silent that Lida wondered if she wasn't pregnant. The electrician sent by the apartment-house management committee to do repairs had been to prison—for a crime just short of murder, it turned out. In short, all people were interesting, if you could get to know them.

By education, Lida was a specialist in medical hygiene. Now she reviewed her classmates one by one. Pavinski, Rozhin, Yankelevich, Theofanov . . . Mishchenko, it seems, had gone into sports. Levin had gone into science. Levin, Boris Levin, a professor, brainy, a Doctor of Sciences . . . They said he had been to France.

Agapova took out a notepad and wrote on a clean sheet: "Levin."

Then she started going over her husband's friends—also, of course, interesting people. Economists. Kalinin, for example, always insisted that unemployment was the chief stimulus to progress. As things stand, every worker knows he won't be fired. And if he does get fired, it's not a big problem: he just goes across the road and gets a job in the neighboring factory. Which means that everyone feels free to take off from work or abuse his position . . . No, Kalinin will hardly be suitable. He's too progressive. And Ilya Merkin is another one. If he's asked what could bring about an upturn in the economy, he answers, "War. War and only war. War is discipline, consciousness-raising. War writes off any shortcomings whatsoever." I'm afraid Merkin won't do either. But wasn't there someone who dropped by the other day—a philologist with a journalist girlfriend? Or maybe he was even a translator. He had served, he said, as a guard escorting prisoners—a convoy overseer. He told us terrible things. His name wasn't Russian: Alikhanov. No doubt an interesting man.

So alongside "Levin" on the notepad she wrote "Alikhanov."

It would be good to have a third candidate. Here Lida remembered that her neighbors had a relative staying with them. Someone from Porkhov. Or else a friend. Mila Osinskaya had mentioned something in the courtyard. There was something mysterious about his past. Maybe he had been arrested, or maybe it was the other way around . . . A boss from the provinces—there was something intriguing about that. She could give it an unusual lead: "There is no geographical provincialism, there is only spiritual provincialism."

So below "Levin" and "Alikhanov" a question mark appeared, and after it "(relative of Mila O.)."

She could also keep as a reserve the well-read building superintendent, who was a great fan of Simenon. Except that he and Lida were always arguing about the overflowing garbage bins . . . Fine. It was time to get things moving.

"Goodbye, Verochka, boys!"

"Agapova, stop in again soon. Don't disappear!"

She called Boris Levin at the clinic. He recognized her voice, seemed pleased, and they arranged to meet at one o'clock.

Alikhanov, the former convoy overseer, turned out to be at home. "Come over," he said. "And if possible, buy three bottles of beer. I'll pay you right back."

Lida stopped at a food store on Karya Street and bought the beer. The buildings in the region were all new projects, and from one entrance to another it was at least a kilometer.

Alikhanov was waiting for her at the door. He was a huge young man with a low forehead and a weak chin. There was a phony Neapolitan glitter in his eyes. He started a kind of senseless, illiterate declamation that he couldn't finish.

"To what do I owe, Lidochka, on what fair wind, which, which . . . Did you get the beer? Smart girl. Take off your coat. This place is an incredible mess."

The room did make a terrible impression. A sofa buried under papers and cigarette ashes. A table invisible beneath a pile of books. The black skeleton of a pre-war typewriter. Some kind of rusty saber on the wall. Unwashed dishes, crimson sediment in the wineglasses. Colorless slabs of herring on a piece of newspaper.

"Come over here. At least it's more or less clean."

"Yes, it's a colorful room," Lida said. "I was trained as a hygienist, you know."

"I received a summons for anti-sanitary conditions from the Civilian Community Court."

"What happened?"

"Nothing. I pleaded a rebellious spirit. I'm a poet, I said, a yogi, a Buddhist. Naturally I live in filth . . . Would you like some beer?"

"I don't drink."

"Here's the money. A ruble eleven."

"What nonsense!" Lida said.

"No, pardon me," Alikhanov protested loudly.

Lida put the handful of change into her pocket. The overseer deftly opened one of the beers, and drank right from the bottle.

"That's better," he confided. And then he tried once more, this time with an assault of words, to overcome the unwieldy sentence. "To what do I owe, so to speak, this unexpected pleasure which . . . ?"

"Are you a philologist?" Agapova asked.

"To be more exact, I'm a linguist. I'm working on the problem of the phonematics of the letter *shchah*."

"That's a problem?"

"One of the liveliest . . . Listen, what happened? To whom do I owe the unexpected pleasure of beholding with my own eyes . . . ?"

The overseer emptied the second bottle.

"We're preparing a radio broadcast, 'A Meeting with an

Interesting Person.' We need a subject with an unusual life story. You're a philologist. To be more exact, a linguist. A former convoy overseer. A man with a many-leveled life . . . Do you have a life with many levels?"

"Recently, yes," Alikhanov answered honestly.

"Tell me in detail about your philological research. But in simple language, so that a layman could understand."

"I'd rather give you one of my papers to read. Somehow I'm not thinking very clearly at the moment. It's around here somewhere. I'll find it in a minute."

Alikhanov rushed to the stratified heap of papers.

"Another time," Lida said, trying to calm him. "Obviously we'll meet again. This is just the preliminary interview. I would like to ask you something. You were a convoy overseer. Wasn't that very dangerous and risky?"

Alikhanov thought about it reluctantly.

"There were some risks, of course. We drank a lot of vodka. We wouldn't have turned down after-shave lotion. All that has to affect the heart."

"No, I mean, the prisoners. After all, they're terrible people. There's nothing sacred to them."

"They're people like other people," Alikhanov said, opening the third bottle.

"I've read a great deal about it. It's a special world. With its own laws . . . Courage is an absolute requirement. Are you a brave man?"

Alikhanov became completely unnerved. "Luba," he said.

"Lida."

"Lida!" he almost shouted. "I'll go get six rubles. I have humane neighbors. Let's get a half-bottle and some dry wine. I can't think quite clearly, somehow."

"I don't drink. Are you a brave man?"

"I don't know. There was a time when I could drink two liters. Now I get silly after seven hundred grams. It must be age . . ."

"You don't understand. I need someone original, an interesting personality. You're a philologist, a man of delicate emotions and fine intelligence. But before that you were a convoy overseer. You had to take risks every day. Spiritual delicacy is often thrown together with physical crudeness."

"When was I ever crude with you?"

"Not with me. But you stood watch over prisoners."

"It would be more correct to say we stood watch over ourselves."

"Where did you get that scar? And don't be modest."

"It's not a scar," Alikhanov exclaimed. "I had a boil. I scratched it. Forgive me."

"All the same, I want to know what you experienced in the north. To put it figuratively, what was the tundra silent about?"

"What?"

"What was the tundra silent about?"

"Lida!" Alikhanov cried wildly. "I can't take this any more! I'm not suitable for a radio broadcast! Yesterday I got drunk! I have debts and alimony to pay! My name has been mentioned on the German radio! I'm a sort of dissident! You'll be fired . . . Let me go."

Lida screwed on the cap of her fountain pen. "It's too bad," she said. "The material is interesting. Be well. I'll call you. And meanwhile look for that paper."

The overseer stood up, pale and exhausted. "Just a minute," he said. "I'll come out with you. I have humane neighbors."

They parted on the landing. Lida walked downstairs. Alikhanov rushed up to the fourth floor.

Levin put his arms around her and looked at her for a long time. "Yes," he said, "the years are going by, the years are going by . . ."

"Have I aged?"

"How shall I put it? You've taken shape."

"And you've gotten flabby. Shame on you. Is Galina home?"

"She's at a school meeting. We have a little hooligan who's growing up. You say I'm getting fat? My wife says to me, 'You should run every morning.' And I tell her, 'If I start running, I won't come back.' Would you like some coffee? Take off your things."

"Only after you, Doctor," Lida said, reminded of an old joke.

They went into the living room. A big standing lamp with a burnt lampshade. Foreign journals on the window-sill.

"This is a good apartment," Lida said. "New apartments usually make me uncomfortable. Everything lacquered, crystal all over the place . . ."

"I have crystal too," Levin boasted.

"Where?"

"In hock."

"Are you still working on carcinogens?"

"Still the same."

"Tell me about it."

"Just a minute. I'll put the kettle on."

"I'll be waiting."

Lida took out a notebook, fountain pen, and a pack of "BT" cigarettes.

Levin returned. They lit up.

"You were in France."

"Two weeks."

"So, how was it?"

"Normal."

"Could you be more specific?"

"A hard-working people, a reactionary bourgeoisie, economic crisis, impoverishment of the masses . . ."

"Talk like a human being. Do the French like us?"

"Who the hell knows? They're all in a good mood."

"What about the high standard of living? How did you like French women?"

"The standard of living is normal. The food was good. I was fed exclusively dietetic food: wine, young chickens, coffee, cream. The girls are wonderful. Or rather, they're either very ugly or beauties. I figure it's all a matter of cosmetics. Cosmetics bring out the good features and underline the bad ones. Their manner is free and direct. They all wore these white synthetic smocks, low cut . . ."

"What do you mean, 'white smocks'? Did you work in a clinic?"

"I didn't work. I came down with dysentery in Nice. I walked around for a day and then was hospitalized."

"Which is to say, practically speaking, you didn't see France?"

"No, why? We had a color television in the hospital."

"That was bad luck, getting sick."

"But at least I had a good rest."

"Did you bring home anything interesting? Any souvenirs, or something to wear?"

"Listen," Levin said, livening up. "I brought home something unique. Only if I show it to you, don't be sanctimonious. After all, you've had medical training. I'll go find it. I have to hide it from Tolya, my son."

"What are you talking about?"

"Lida, I brought home a penis. A filigreed rubber penis. I swear to you. Where has it gotten to? Apparently Galina has hidden it somewhere."

"What do you need that for?"

"What do you mean, 'what for'? It's a work of art. I swear. And Galka likes it too."

"How did you get it through customs?"

"Obviously I didn't carry it in my hands. I hid it."

"Where? It's not exactly a needle."

"I asked a woman who works in our lab. Women are searched less carefully. Besides, they have more possibilities . . ."

"You're like a child. We'd better talk business."

"In a minute. I'll get the coffee."

Candies, sugar wafers, and a lemon appeared on the table.

"Can I get you some condensed milk?"

"No. Go on, tell me more about yourself."

"What is there to tell? I'm working on the construction of models of chemical reactions. At one time I did research on the carcinogenic properties of asbestos dust."

"Tell me, is there a cure for cancer?"

"Cancer of the skin, yes."

"And cancer of the stomach, for example?"

"Lidochka, there's complete chaos in terms of opinion on the subject. A milligram of a carcinogen can kill a horse. Any grown man has on his finger enough of the very same carcinogens to poison a herd. I sit here and smoke, yet I'm still alive. Smoke is another one of them . . . Don't bother taking notes. Cancer is too touchy a subject. They'll turn it down if you propose it."

"I don't think so."

"What, you don't think I've dealt with journalists before? Better ask some general practitioner for an interview. They have an easy life, signing social pledges every month. Call your office, and see if they don't agree."

Agapova called Nina Ignatyevna and told her about Levin. "Lidochka," Nina Ignatyevna said, suddenly very uneasy, "cancer is too sad a subject. It engenders negative emotions. It calls up associations with a certain notorious banned novel. We expect something on the brighter side."

"But cancer is problem number one."

"Lidochka, don't get stubborn. There are certain unspoken rules."

"Well then," Lida sighed, "sorry."

"Where are you going?" Levin said in surprise. "Stay a while longer."

"I really stopped by on business."

"We haven't seen each other in seven years. Galka will be home soon. We'll have something to drink."

"Please forgive me. I don't feel like seeing her."

Levin was silent.

"Are you happy, Borya?"

Levin took off his glasses. Now he looked like a schoolboy who had been kept back a year.

"What's the use of talking about happiness! I live, I work. Galina is a difficult person, I agree. There's something lifeless about her. And Tolya is a boor—a well-read, well-educated boor. I am, after all, a Doctor of Sciences, a full professor. Yesterday he says to me, 'You have an inferiority complex.' "

"But still, you're a scientist, you serve humanity. You must feel proud of yourself . . ."

"Stop it, Lida. I serve Galina and that little shit."

"You're just in a bad mood." By now Lida was standing outside the open door.

"But do you remember the time we went to Novgorod?" Levin asked.

"Borya, let's close the subject right now. Everything turned out for the best. Well, I'm off."

She walked downstairs, opening her umbrella as she went. A click, and over her head a many-colored, slightly vibrating cupola took shape.

"And remember the time we stole melons?" he shouted down the stairwell.

By now it had grown dark. The puddles swam with watercolor neon lights. The pale faces of passersby all seemed aloof. A brightly lit tram, rocking from side to side, pulled around the corner. Lida sat down on a wooden seat. Folded her umbrella. The dark windowpane across from her reflected her tired face. She held out her money to someone, and a ticket was shoved back. She slept all the way home and awoke with a headache. She walked home slowly, stepping in puddles. Good thing she had had the foresight to wear her Czech rubber boots.

The Osinskys lived in the other wing of her building. Arkady was an athletics coach, always joking. Under the suede jacket, a stopwatch shone on his chest. Mila taught chemistry somewhere.

Their son was a mysterious individual. For six years he had been avoiding military service. For six years he had alternately pretended to have neuroses, a stomach ulcer, and chronic arthritis. In his ailments he outdid the legendary revolutionary Kamo. By the end of those years he had become genuinely nervous, ruined his digestive system, and acquired chronic arthritis. As far as medical learning went, Igor had long since outstripped all the district doctors. Besides that, he had a good knowledge of jazz and spoke English fluently.

In general, a rather interesting person. But he didn't work.

Lida climbed the stairs to the third floor. Suddenly, uncontrollably, she wanted to go home. She drove the thought away and pressed the doorbell. Milord's muffled barking could be heard through the door.

"Come in," Mila said, very pleased she had come. "Igor's off running around somewhere. Arik is at a training camp in Matsesta. Come meet Vladimir Ivanovich."

As she entered the room, a heavy-set man of about sixty rose to greet her. He held out his hand and introduced himself. With dignity, he poured some cognac. Mila turned on the television.

"Would you like some borscht?"

"No. Strange as it may seem, I would like a drink."

"To all the best," Vladimir Ivanovich proposed amicably.

He was a broad-shouldered, healthy man, wearing a handsome, finely knit sweater. The face of a man who drinks regularly but in moderation. In films, his type always plays the retired colonel. A solid forehead, the usual blue eyes, gold caps on his teeth.

They touched glasses and drank.

"Well, have a talk," the hostess said, "and I'll just run over to the Vorobyovs for ten minutes. Rita's knitting me a sweater."

And she left.

"I've really come on business," Lida said.

"I'm at your disposal."

"We're preparing a radio broadcast called 'A Meeting with an Interesting Person.' Ludmila Sergeyevna once told me something about you. And I thought . . . It seems to me that you are an interesting person."

"I'm a most ordinary person," Vladimir Ivanovich said, "although, to be frank, I like my work and am respected by the collective."

"Where do you work?" Lida took out her notebook.

"In Porkhov we have a branch of the Red Dawn Factory. We construct sized coordinates for pay telephones. Our factory shop is large and prominent. According to the results of the second quarter, we have attained significant successes . . ."

"Aren't you bored?"

"I don't understand."

"Isn't it boring, living in a provincial town?"

"Our city is growing, being improved with more services and utilities. We have a new House of Culture, a stadium, housing projects . . . Did you write that down?"

Vladimir Ivanovich tipped the bottle toward her. Lida shook her head. He drank, speared a slippery marinated mushroom with his fork.

After a moment, Lida continued. "I think it's possible to be a provincial in the capital and an urban sophisticate on the tundra."

"Absolutely right."

"I mean to say, the provinces are a spiritual phenomenon and not a geographical one."

"Exactly the point. What's more, we have a fine supply of produce: meat, fish, vegetables . . ."

"Do performing groups come there on tour from the capital?"

"That goes without saying. Even Magomayev himself comes."

Vladimir Ivanovich poured himself another cognac.

"Of course you read a great deal?" Lida asked.

"How can one do without it? I value Simonov, Ananiev, war memoirs, naturally the classics: Pushkin, Lermontov, Tolstoy. There were three writers by the last-mentioned name, as is well known . . . In my youth I wrote poetry."

"That's interesting."

"God help my memory. Here, for example:

> *Each of us strives to be a hero,*
> *As brothers we march in the ranks;*
> *In Stalin's name we shall spread o'er the earth,*
> *In battle obtain joy and thanks.*

Lida suppressed a wave of disappointment.

"Is it hard to be the head of a shop section?"

"I'll be blunt. It's not easy. There are certain factors of production, but also moral factors . . . The plan, labor turnover, the microclimate, those who retard production. But the main thing is, the people have become demanding. They know their rights. Give them this, give them that . . . No obligations at all, and rights from here down to hell. Ech, old man Stalin is no more . . . *Then* there was order, order. If you were late to work by a minute, you got arrested! While now . . . The people have gotten soft, gotten soft. Satirists, you understand, all around us . . . Ech, the old man's gone . . ."

"Does that mean that you approve of the cult of personality?" Agapova asked quietly.

"Cult, cult . . . The cult exists and will exist . . . A personality is necessary, you understand—a personality!"

Vladimir Ivanovich had gotten heated up and slightly drunk. Now he gesticulated, leaned over the table and waved his fork.

"It's not an easy life I've lived. I've seen all sorts of things. I've fallen low, I've flown up high . . . After all, I was, just between us, married."

"Why just between us?" Lida asked, surprised.

"To Yakir's niece," Vladimir Ivanovich added in a whisper.

"Yakir? *The* Yakir?"

"The same. We had a child, a little boy . . ."

"And where are they now?"

"I don't know. I lost track of them. That was in 1939 . . ."

Vladimir Ivanovich became silent and withdrew into his own thoughts.

Lida waited for a long time. Then, fearfully, blushing, she asked, "That is . . . How is that, 'lost track of them'? How does someone lose track of his wife? How do you lose track of your own child?"

"Those were harsh times, Lidochka—harsh and stormy times. Families were broken up, the age-old foundations of society broken up—"

"What have the age-old foundations of society got to do with it?" Lida cried out suddenly. "I'm not a child, I know everything. They arrested Yakir, and you basely abandoned your wife and son. You . . . You . . . You . . . are not an interesting person!"

"I would ask you," Vladimir Ivanovich said. "I would ask you . . . Such words should not be thrown about lightly . . ."

And then, already amicable again, "You should behave more modestly, Lidochka. More modestly, more modestly . . ."

Milord lifted his head.

Lida was not listening any longer. She jumped up, grabbed her jacket hanging in the entryway, and slammed the door.

On the stairs it was quiet and cold. An unseen cat scurried by like a shadow. The smell of frying fish wafted behind it a feeling of misery.

Lida walked downstairs and across the courtyard. A damp twilight had hidden itself beyond the garages and around the garbage bins. The branches of the uncared-for city shrubs stood out darkly and rasped in the wind. A toy horse had been left in the snow.

Lida looked in her mailbox and pulled out *The Economic Gazette*. Climbed the stairs and unlocked the door. In her husband's room the television was humming. Tania's red between-season coat hung on the coatrack. Lida took off her coat and threw down her gloves on the little table under the mirror.

With hardly any sign of greeting, a young man slipped past her into the bathroom. His dirty curls were tied back with a brown shoelace. His velvet trousers trailed behind him like the train of a dress.

"Tatiana, who's that?" Lida asked.

"Suppose it's Zhenia. We're studying together."

"Studying what?"

"Suppose it's German. Do you have any objection?"

"Make sure he washes his hands," Lida said.

"You always love to vulgarize everything!" her daughter said in a whisper full of hatred.

Lida called me at one in the morning. Her voice sounded agitated and muffled.

"I didn't wake you?" she asked.

"No," I said. "It's worse than that."

"You're not alone?"

"Alone. With Marina."

"Can you talk seriously for a moment?"

"Of course."

"Surely within your entire range of acquaintances you know one interesting person?"

"I do. He sends you his regards."

"Stop it. This is a very serious matter. I have to write a script by Thursday."

"About what?"

"A meeting with an interesting person. Do you have a suitable candidate for me?"

"Lida," I begged. "After all, you know what kind of people my friends are. They're all bums. Call Klensky, he has a father-in-law who's an invalid."

"I have a proposition. You and I will write a script together. We'll each make fifteen rubles."

"But I don't know how to use a tape recorder."

"I'll take charge of that. I need your—"

"Cynicism?"

"Your professional experience," Lida said tactfully.

"Fine," I said, to get out of the conversation. "I'll call you in the morning. Rather, later today."

"Only promise, please, that you'll call."

"I just said I would . . ."

Here Marina couldn't stand it any longer and bit my finger.

"Till tomorrow," I said, or rather shouted, and hung up.

Lida opened the door to her husband's room, which was filled with blue light. Vadim was lying on the sofa, wearing his shoes.

"May I finally get some supper?" he asked.

Her daughter appeared in the doorway. "We're going out." Tania's face was gloomy, her features set in a grimace of eternal rebellion.

"Come back soon."

"May I finally have some tea, please?" Vadim asked.

"I work too, by the way," Lida answered. And then, not allowing the argument to escalate, she said, "What do you think—is Ilya Merkin an interesting person?"

THE SEVENTH COMPROMISE

("Soviet Estonia." April 1976.)
APPAREL FOR A MARTIAN (People and Professions).

What do we expect from a good tailor? A suit he cuts should keep to the current fashion. So what would you think of a tailor whose creations lag behind the current style by 200 years? What is more, this man commands great respect and merits the warmest praise. We speak here of the cutter-modeler of the Russian Drama Theater of the Estonian Republic, Voldemar Sild. Among his regular clients one finds Spanish grandees and French musketeers, Russian tsars and Japanese samurai—and what is more, vixens, roosters, and even Martians.

A theatrical costume is born out of the joint efforts of the artistic director and the tailor. It has to correspond to the nature of the era while also expressing the spirit of the performance and the attributes of the individual characters. Imagine Onegin dressed in baggy pants, or Sobakevich in an elegant tailcoat! When he had to create a costume for the character of Aesop the slave, Voldemar Sild studied ancient painting and Greek drama.

The frockcoat, caftan, military cloak, pelisse, smock frock—these are all absolutely distinct types of clothing, each with its own specific features and accessories.

"I remember one young actor," Sild relates, "who asked me if there was really any difference between a tailcoat and a smoking jacket. To me they are as different as a television set and a tape recorder."

When he attends performances at other theaters, Voldemar Hendrikovich, with typical professional severity, gives his attention to the way the characters are outfitted. "And only at performances of my beloved Vakhtangov Theater," says Voldemar Sild, "do I forget that I'm a modeler and get absorbed in the action of the play—which is a true sign that the dress designer of that theater does impeccable work."

Voldemar Sild does impeccable work himself, as tailor, artist, and man of the theater.

At the unofficial editorial board meeting, my article drew quite a bit of praise.

"Dovlatov can write vividly about any sort of nonsense."

"And his headline is effective."

"And the words he comes up with! 'Accessories . . .' "

The next day, Chief Editor Turonok called me in. "Sit down."

I sat.

"This conversation will not be pleasant."

Like all conversations with you, you idiot, I thought.

"What is the heading of the column you wrote this for?"

" 'People and Professions.' We look for people in rare professions, and also unexpected angles."

"Do you know the profession of this Mr. Sild of yours?"

"Of course. He's a tailor. A theatrical tailor. That's the unexpected angle."

"That's now. And earlier?"

"I don't know what he did earlier."

"Then you should know that during the war he was an executioner. He served under the Germans. He hanged Soviet patriots. For which he served twelve years in prison."

"Oh Lord!" I said.

"Do you realize what you've done? You have honored a betrayer of the Motherland! You have damaged the reputation of an interesting column forever!"

"But he was recommended to me by the director of the theater."

"The director of the theater was a former S.S. lieutenant. Besides that, he's blue."

"What does that mean—'blue'?"

"That was what homosexuals used to be called. Didn't he make a pass at you?"

"Make a pass at me? And how. He shook my hand. And me a journalist. Was I surprised."

At that moment, I remembered a conversation with a certain Frenchman. We were talking about homosexuality.

"You can be prosecuted for practicing it in this country," I boasted.

"How about for having hemorrhoids? Do they prosecute you for that too?" the Frenchman growled.

"I don't really blame you," Turonok said. "You acted in a proper way. That is, you wrote an article on the director's recommendation. But all the same, one should be more circumspect. The choice of a hero is a serious matter—extraordinarily serious."

Everyone at the office talked about this incident for about two weeks. Then my colleague Bush distinguished himself. He wrote up an interview with the captain of a West German merchant marine ship. It was the eve of the anniversary of the October Revolution. Bush's captain praised the Soviet regime. Then someone found out that the captain was in fact an Estonian defector. He had made it out to Finland by canoe in the summer of 1969, then gone from there to Sweden. And so on. Bush had invented the interview from beginning to end. That incident had repercussions, and everyone forgot about me.

THE EIGHTH COMPROMISE

("Soviet Estonia." June 1976.)
TALLINN BIDS FAREWELL TO HUBERT ILVES. Yesterday at the Linnamets Cemetery a true son of the Estonian Republic was buried, the permanent director of the television studio and a Hero of Socialist Labor, Hubert Voldemarovich Ilves.

The entire life of Hubert Ilves was a model of selfless devotion to the cause of Communism.

He was distinguished by an unwavering sense of responsibility, attention to his fellow workers, and an extraordinary personal modesty.

To the strains of the funeral march, leading representatives of the public community carried the wreath-covered coffin containing the body of the deceased.

Above the open grave the solemn words of leave-taking resounded.

Taking part in the funeral ceremonies were leading Party and Soviet activists, colleagues of the deceased, fellow-workers in radio and television, and the major Estonian newspapers.

The memory of Hubert Ilves will live eternally in our hearts.

"Comrade Dovlatov, do you have a black suit?"

Turonok frowned with displeasure. He was uncomfortable asking such a personal question of an employee of the republic Party newspaper. Looking at him now, with his beige-colored, infantile face and wide waist, I realized that his name always reminded me of a baby animal.

"No," I said. "I have a sweater."

"Not here, I mean at home."

"Actually, I don't own a suit," I said.

I could have also explained that I don't have a home or refuge or even an address. That I rent a room, God knows where . . .

"Then how do you attend the theater?"

I could have explained that I don't attend the theater. But the newspaper had just published my review of a production of *The Dowerless Girl*. I based it on Dima Sher's description. The review had been praised for its polemical nature.

"However, let's get down to the heart of the matter," the editor said wearily. "Ilves has passed away."

By force of my foul habit of lying, my face took on an expression of sorrow.

"You knew him?" the editor asked.

"No," I said.

"Ilves was the director of the television studio. His funeral is a serious undertaking. I hope I'm making myself clear?"

"Yes."

"A person from our editorial staff has to be present. We wanted to send Shablinsky."

"Right move," I said. "Mishka is always doing hack-work for them."

Turonok frowned. "Mikhail Borisovich is busy. He's being sent on assignment to Saaremaa Island. Klensky is out of the question. We need a man of imposing appearance. Bush is on a binge, and so forth. We have settled on you as our choice. I beg you, don't let us down. It will be necessary to give a short, heartfelt speech. It's crucial that . . . In general, behave as though you knew the deceased intimately."

"Can you really say I have an imposing appearance?"

"You're tall," Turonok said condescendingly. "I talked this over with Klyukhina."

Ah, I thought, Galochka. But that's all right.

"Henry Franzovich," I said, "I don't like this. It smells of a hoax. I didn't know Ilves. I don't want to fake mourning. Better send Shablinsky. And I, if need be, will go to Saaremaa."

"Out of the question. You don't produce topical articles."

"They don't assign me any, so I don't produce them."

"You were assigned a piece on the Germans living in Estonia, and you refused."

"I think they should be allowed to leave."

"You're a naïve person. To put it mildly."

"Why? In the Union there are more Germans than Armenians. But they haven't even been granted their own autonomy."

"But what kind of Germans are they? Third-generation colonists. They became Estonians long ago in their language, culture, their way of thinking. They're typical Estonians. Their fathers and grandfathers lived in Estonia . . ."

"The grandfather of Boris Roiblat also lived in Estonia. And his father too. But Borya remains a Jew all the same. And remains unemployed."

"You know, Dovlatov, it's impossible to talk with you. You have certain demagogic ways of arguing. We gave you work, met you halfway. We thought you'd mature, that you'd conduct yourself a little more respectably."

"Well, I work. I write."

"And you don't write badly either. Yurna himself quoted one of your lines not long ago: 'A constructive idea has been lost in the chaos of an irresponsible experiment.' But I'm talking about something else. Your apolitical stand, your infantilism . . . You can always be counted on to act out of step. You make two hundred and fifty rubles a month. You're well regarded, your humor and style are appreciated. The question is: What do you give back in return? Why do I have to waste time on these fruitless conversations? I ask you most urgently to take Shablinsky's place. He will give you his jacket, temporarily. Try it on. It's there, on the coatrack."

I tried it on.

"Some lapels," I said. "All they need right here is an Order of the Red Banner."

"That's all," the editor interrupted. "Go."

I hate graveside ceremonies. Not because someone has died, since as it happens I've never had to bury anyone I was close to. And to anyone else I'm indifferent. Still, I hate funerals. Against the background of someone's death, any movement seems immoral. I hate funerals for their tone of beautiful, convincing sorrow. For the tears from people who are really strangers, alien mourners. For the suppressed feeling of gladness: "You didn't die, it was somebody else." For the secret excitement about the drinking that will follow. For the exaggerated compliments addressed to the deceased. (I have always wanted to shout, "He couldn't care less! Be more tolerant of the living. Of me, for example.")

And now, stepping in for Shablinsky, I was supposed to take part in the funeral solemnities, to grieve and play the hypocrite. I called the television studio.

"Who's in charge of the funeral?"

"Ilves himself."

I almost fell off my chair.

"Rando Ilves, the son of the deceased. And the organizing committee."

"How can I get in touch with them? I'll write down the number . . . Thanks."

I called. Someone with a heavy Baltic accent answered.

"Are you a relative of the deceased?"

"A colleague."

"You work for TV?"

"Yes."

"Your name is Shablinsky, right?"

I nearly said yes. "Shablinsky is away on assignment. I've been asked to take his place."

"We're waiting for you. Third floor, Room Twelve."

"I'm on my way."

Room 12 was crowded with people wearing armbands. I didn't know anyone there. Shablinsky's jacket, faithful to the contours of his body, was tight and constricting on mine. I felt awkward: a dead whale in a swimming pool. A horse in a dog house.

(I've slowed down, trying to catch the right metaphor.)

A woman sitting at a desk called out to me, "Are you Shablinsky?"

"No."

"*Soviet Estonia* was supposed to send a Shablinsky."

"He's away on assignment. I've been sent to replace him."

"I see. Is the text of your speech ready?"

"What text? I thought that would be . . . an emotional improvisation."

"There are regulations. Approval of the text is strictly required."

"Can I give it to you tomorrow?"

"Spare yourself the trouble. Here is the text Shablinsky prepared."

"Great," I said. "Thanks."

I was handed two sheets of onionskin. On them I read: "Comrades! How I envy Ilves! Yes, yes, don't be surprised. I am gripped by a feeling of pure envy. What a rich life he had! What impressive achievements! What enviable glory was won by this dreamer and fighter!"

Next came the list of his merits and services. And then, for the finale: "Sleep, Hubert Ilves! You rarely had enough sleep. Sleep!"

Reading all this was absolutely out of the question. On paper I can say anything. But out loud, in front of people . . .

I turned to the woman at the desk.

"I would like to bring in something of my own, to change it just a little. I'm not as emotional . . ."

"You'll have to keep the basic form. It's been approved."

"Of course."

"Copy over the data."

I copied it down.

"There's not supposed to be any ad-libbing."

"You know," I said, "ad-libbing has to be better than his-libbing."

"What?" the woman asked.

"Fine," I said. "Everything will go as normal."

Now a few words about Shablinsky. His father was arrested during the purges. His uncle, a professor, is mentioned in Nadezhda Mandelstam's memoirs. He's practically the only person the author speaks of kindly.

Misha grew up in a dreary camp settlement. He was taught arithmetic and grammar by the leading lights of Soviet science —all of them wearing the quilted jackets of prisoners. It was in this environment that his conceptions of life were formed. He grew up to be sturdy and sensible. He didn't trust words, and he always acted decisively. Read a lot. An interest in poetry and a love of technology coexisted within him. Before he had a diploma he worked as a construction engineer. Then he went through university training. Became a journalist specializing in industry. From then on, his sphere was to be a hybrid of poetry and technology.

He was ready to do anything for the sake of reaching a goal. He would use any means. Then the goals themselves became more and more cloudy. Life became a struggle to get at the means. The alternative of good and evil was transformed into the alternative of success and failure. His worldly activities started slowing his moral growth. By the time I met him he was a typical newspaperman—duplicitous and cynical. There's a remarkable saying about journalists attributed to Henry Ford: "An honest journalist only sells out once." However, I consider this statement to be idealistic. Journalism has its perpetually open markets, commissioned stories, and even flea markets. Which is to say, the selling-out is always going on, full blast.

There is a life which is magnificent, tortured, and full of tragedy. And then there's work, which is well paid. Work for which you create a different, more distinct, tragedy-free, harmonious life. On paper.

A journalist sits and writes. "It was the fateful year 1919 . . ."

He stops for a moment and yells to his tiresome wife, "Garik Lerner promised to get me three jars of instant coffee."

And his wife yells back from the kitchen, "What? They haven't put Lerner in jail yet?"

But his pen is already scratching on. Something like: "Yet another mystery has been stolen from nature." Or: "In New York, gillyflowers have no fragrance."

The life of a journalist contains all the elements that grace the life of any worthy man.

Sincerity? A journalist says sincerely what he doesn't believe.

Creativity? A journalist creates endlessly, passing off the desired as the actual.

Love? A journalist loves tenderly what is not worth loving.

However, we're off the track.

From the television studio I went to Marina's. For a whole year, something had been going on between us on the order of an intellectual intimacy. With shades of animosity and sex.

Marina worked in the secretarial department of our newspaper. Before and after work her behavior was governed by the skepticism and rather crude directness of a thirty-year-old unmarried woman.

Once she had been Shablinsky's girlfriend. Like every other woman who worked in our office. All of them, without exception, sooner or later gave in to his advances. For a long time the secret of his successes was unclear to me. Then I understood what it was. Shablinsky conquered with the unambiguousness of his advances. For example, he announced to a student field-worker from Lithuania, with whom he was barely acquainted, "I love you. And even the possibility of the clap won't stop me."

Once I said to him, "Mishka, I'm not a prig. But you're involved with four ladies. New Year's Eve is coming. You can't, after all, ask all four of them out."

"Why not?" Shablinsky asked.

"There could be a terrible scene."

"That's not excluded as a possibility," he said, growing thoughtful.

"So what are you going to do?"

Shablinsky thought a while, sighed, and said, "If you only knew what a serious problem it is . . ."

He broke up with Marina because he decided to get married. Marina wasn't suitable as a bride. She was, I repeat, around thirty, she smoked, and she knew a lot. Misha was interested in the traditional Jewish-marriage variety. Young virgin with housekeeping tendencies. Someone introduced him to one. The very thing—sweet Rozochka with the fuzzy upper lip. She read, could understand things . . . A merchant papa . . .

Roza blinked her eyes and kept repeating, "Oy, how could I get married? After all, I have no experience of it . . ."

"What is it you haven't got?" Shablinsky guffawed.

So he left Marina. And that was where I turned up. Pensive, polite, honest. And it was as if she saw me for the first time. For the first time appreciated me.

There's a certain interesting feature to my virtues. They blossom and become apparent only against the backdrop of some kind of disgraceful behavior. So I'm liked by rejected ladies.

At the beginning she talked about Shablinsky all the time.

"You know, he obviously loved me in his own way. Once I reproached him: 'You don't love me!' What do you suppose he did? Took my clothes and handbag and hung them."

"Where?" I asked.

"You don't know what I'm saying? This was at night. Complete intimacy. I said: 'You don't love me!' And he took my clothes and bag and hung them. On his thing. To show how strong he was. And how much he loved me."

And so, from the television studio I was on my way to Marina's. The house she lived in was in a neighborhood of new housing projects reserved for colleagues from the newspaper. You get off the trolleybus and there's a vacant lot, a huge building, and in every window a co-worker.

I walked to the fourth floor and rang her bell. And just then I remembered that I was wearing Shablinsky's jacket. The door was thrown open. Marina stared at me in surprise. Maybe she thought I had cut Shablinsky's throat out of jealousy and stolen his jacket.

(Women have a kind of supernatural memory when it comes to clothing. My wife once said of someone, "Yes, you know him. You know him perfectly well. Such an unpleasant man, in black shoes with brown shoelaces.")

A good man's dealings with women are always fraught with difficulties. And I am a good man. I can say this without the slightest embarrassment, because it's nothing to be proud of. People expect a good man to behave accordingly. He is faced with high demands. He loads himself down each day with the excruciating burden of nobility, intelligence, diligence, conscience, and humor. Then he gets rejected in favor of an out-and-out creep. And the creep gets told, with much laughter, all about the boring virtues of the good man.

Women only love scoundrels, as everyone knows. However, it is not given to everyone to be a scoundrel. I knew a man, a currency speculator, called "The Shark." He used to beat his wife with the haft of a shovel. Took her imported shampoo and gave it as a gift to his mistress. Killed the cat. Once in his life he made his wife a cheese sandwich. All that night she lay and sobbed, her heart overflowing with gratitude and tenderness. After he was arrested, she sent him cans of food to a Mordovian prison camp for nine years. And waited for him.

But a good man—who needs him, I'd like to know?

So there I was, in somebody else's jacket.

"What's the matter?" Marina said, seeing in this change of clothes some sort of sexual outrage. Some sort of insulting interchangeability of emotions.

"This is Misha's jacket," I said. "Temporarily, so that I look respectable."

"Maybe you want to propose to me?" (Humor with a touch of gall.)

"If I were serious, I'd do it simply."

"Don't be afraid."

"I have to speak at a funeral. Ilves died."

"Ilves? From the TV studio? How awful . . . Have you eaten?"

"I don't remember. I never saw Ilves face to face."

"There's bouillon and meat patties and duck."

"Good, let's eat. Shall I run down for some vodka?"

"I have some. There's a little left."

I am well acquainted with the homes of cultured people. Icons, samovars, heads of Nefertiti. Some highly significant shards of broken pottery. A ton of books, all new. And vodka—only a little left. Eternally, only a little left. And where does it come from? Did someone bring it? Why didn't he finish it all? Was he busy with more important matters?

I have no right to be jealous. My wife, alimony . . . It would take a long time to explain. The composition of this story would collapse.

"Where's the vodka from?" I asked. "Who was here?"

I wasn't jealous. I didn't care about the other man. It's just a sort of game between us.

"Edik stopped by. He's depressed."

The person being referred to was the poet Bogatyreyev. An overly long last name, glasses, a deranged way of laughing. I once saw a book of his poems. It was called either *The Hypotenuse of the Good* or else *The Bisection of the Heart*. Something like that. Free verse. Or maybe I'm wrong. Like these lines, for example:

> *We walked side by side, like two tears,*
> *And we could not unite.*

And further the notation: "Night, 21–22 December. On the Leningrad-Tallinn Express."

"He's always depressed. It's his working condition. Just as Bush's working condition is being plastered."

"Don't be mean!"

"Fine . . ."

"Do you want to see what I wrote in my diary? About you?"

Marina brought out a cherry-colored notebook. On the cover in gold letters were the words "To the Delegates of the Tallinn Party Conference."

"Don't read there. And not there. Here it is: 'He was the holiday of my body and the guest of my soul. Night, 19–20 August 1975.' "

I read it and suddenly shuddered. The room filled with unbearable heat. The blue walls were creeping upwards diagonally. The prints on the wall rocked back and forth before my eyes. An attack of choking launched me out the door. Swishing against the wallpaper as I went, I rushed for the bathroom. Leaned against the sink, bowed over the cold porcelain edge. Vomited. Stuck my head under the faucet. Icy water flowed beneath my collar. Out of delicacy, Marina waited in the corridor. Then she asked, "Did you get drunk last night?"

"Oh, don't bother me."

"It's just that it's sad to watch a man's ruin."

"You know," I said, "in our circumstances it may be more fitting to lose than to win."

"You like to feel that you're the underdog. You admire your own failures. You show them off . . ."

"Have you got a lemon?"

"Just a minute."

I sat chewing on the lemon, the expression on my face appropriate. And Marina kept harping on the same note: "Genuine talent eventually cuts a path through for itself. Sooner or later it will happen. Write, work, go after what you want."

"I'm going after it. It even seems I've already got it. I've been reprimanded by an instructor from the Central Committee on cultural affairs. Listen. And where is that stuff? You said there was a little left."

Marina brought out some sort of junk in a foreign bottle, and two tall wineglasses. Turned on the record player. Naturally, Vivaldi. Long associated with heavy drinking.

"You know," I said, "I've dreamed of living among people who act normally with one another."

"I'd like to see you strong, serene, purposeful."

"That means: be like Shablinsky."

"Not at all. Be natural."

"Most likely it's natural for me to be unnatural."

"You complicate everything beyond measure. Being a decent person is not such a big achievement."

"You should try it."

"You don't have to be crude."

And that's true, I thought. What did I say that for? A beautiful woman. All I have to do is stretch out my hand. I stretched it. Shut off the music. Emptied the glass . . .

I heard, "Mishka, I'm about to die!" and a barely discernible tinkling sound. It was Marina, setting the glass down securely with her free, unseen, unnecessary hand.

"Mishka," I said, "is away on assignment."

"Oh Lord!"

I became disgusted and left. To be more honest, I stayed.

By morning the text of my speech was ready.

"Comrades! A sad occasion has brought us here. Hubert Ilves has passed away—a leading administrator, Party member, man of duty . . ." Then came the list of his accomplishments—a slightly fictionalized version of his curriculum vitae. And at the end: "His memory will remain alive in our hearts!"

With this sheet of paper I went to the television studio. There they read it and said, "Somewhat too abstract. However, it's even good that way, as a contrast with the more official speeches."

I called the newspaper office. I was told, "You're to take orders from the funeral commission. Till tomorrow. *Ciao!*"

The funeral commission was dominated by the kind of activity that reminded me of the newsroom atmosphere I knew, with its fake air of preoccupation and high-pitched, feverish ineffectuality. I stood out on the landing next to the fire extinguisher, smoking. It was here that Bykover greeted me. Any newspaper staff will have a kind of non-standard person like him—Jewish, mad, brilliant. Just as any country town has its village idiot. Bykover's history was quite unusual. He was the youngest son of a factory owner in pre-war Tallinn, then known as Revel. He had graduated from Cambridge. Then bourgeois Estonia fell. Like all progressive-minded Jews, Fima was all for the revolution. He joined the foreign department of the republic newspaper. (His knowledge of languages came in handy.) And then one day he was given a highly responsible assignment: to call Dimitrov in Bulgaria and schedule their congratulations on the anniversary of the Estonian Soviet Republic. Bykover called Sofia. Secretary Dimitrov came to the telephone.

"Dis's Tallinn speaking," Bykover announced, retaining his Jewish accent despite all his erudition. "Dis's Tallinn speaking," was how he pronounced it.

In reply he heard: "Dear Comrade Stalin! The freedom-loving people of Bulgaria greet you. Allow me in the name of the workers to report—"

"I'm not Stalin," Bykover corrected him good-naturedly. "I'm Bykover. And I'm calling since, considering the anniversary, it would be nice to organize a short congratulatory item . . . Literally a couple of words . . ."

Forty minutes later, Bykover was arrested. For blasphemous comparison. For desecrating a sacred cause. For imbecility.

After this, much followed. Investigations, a short term in prison camp, then the front, where Bykover once scoured a cow's carcass with sand and chemicals. ("You said to wash it turrily so I did wash it turrily.") Finally he returned. Got a job in some library. He had no degree. (Cambridge didn't count.) They paid him about eighty rubles a month. And meanwhile Bykover had married. His wife was constantly ill but managed to give birth punctually. Poverty-stricken, intimidated, half-crazed, Bykover would hang around the halls of the newspaper office. He would write petty news briefs which had a truly rare poverty of content. "Near the Kalev Factory an elk was seen." "At the home of a retired major, a gigantic cactus has begun to bloom." "The next volume of the complete edition of Grigorovich has just been

THE COMPROMISE

published." And so on. Every day, Bykover would call the maternity hospital to find out whether triplets had been born. Each month, he would review novelties in consumer goods. Each year, it was he who supplied information on the opening of the hunting season. We all liked him.

"Greetings, Fima!" I said in a blasphemously cheerful voice.

"What a misfortune, what a misfortune," Bykover answered.

"They say the deceased was a real operator."

"That's not the word, that's not the word."

"Listen, Fima," I said. "Have you ever tried just once standing up straight or talking in a normal voice?"

Bykover gave me a look that made me blush.

"Do you know what I'd like?" he said. "I would like to become invisible. So that I really didn't exist at all. I would gladly trade places with Ilves, only I have children. Three. And all of them need shoes."

"What are you here for?"

"I didn't want to come. I reasoned like this: Let's suppose Bykover passed away. Would Ilves come to his funeral? Not on your life! So that means I won't go to his. But my wife said, 'Fima, go. Everyone will be there. People who could be useful will be there.'"

"What about me? Am I a useful person?"

"Not very. But you're a good person."

A girl wearing a mourning band looked in.

"Who is Shablinsky?"

"I am," I said.

"Listen. Ilves is in the morgue. He's been properly dressed in a dark blue suit. But it seems his tie is missing. His nephew has just now brought in a tie. Also, someone has to put a Journalists' Union pin on his lapel."

I myself was wearing a tie. It had been given to me a year ago by the currency speculator, "The Shark." Not only that, he had even knotted it for me in an unusual manner. À la Frank Sinatra. From that time on, I had never unknotted it. It worked like this: I would loosen the knot and slowly widen the loop. The tip would remain on the outside of the knot. Then I'd carefully push my head through the loop, flattening my ears. To get the tie off I simply reversed these steps.

"I'm afraid I couldn't manage properly . . ."

"Basically, I know how to do that," Bykover said.

"Wonderful!" the girl said, very pleased. "The truck is waiting downstairs. A chauffeur will drive you, and Altmyae, the sound technician, will go with you. Here's the tie and the union pin. Bring the deceased back here. By that time everyone will be ready. The ceremony will begin at three sharp. And one more thing. Tell Altmyae that the background should show up the contrasts. He'll know what I mean."

We put on our coats and took the elevator downstairs. Bykover said, "I've come in handy for once."

A truck with a van attached to it was parked downstairs. Altmyae, the sound technician, was dozing in the cab.

"Hi, Oscar," I said. "I'm supposed to tell you to remember that the background should show up the contrasts."

"What background now?" Altmyae said, surprised.

"You know."

"What am I supposed to know?"

"The girl asked us to tell you—"

"What girl?"

"Fine," I said. "Go back to sleep."

We climbed into the back of the van. Bykover said happily, "It's a good thing that I can help out. Ilves is a useful person."

"*Who's* a useful person?" I asked, startled.

"The younger Ilves, the son."

"And what does he do?"

"He works in the propaganda department."

"Come sit here," I said. "Closer, where it shakes less."

"It shakes me everywhere the same."

There was a time when I worked as a prison convoy overseer. I escorted prisoners in exactly this kind of metal van. The vehicle was called a "conmobile." Inside, apart from the convoy "salon," the van contained two skinny steel closets. These were called "tumblers." One man could fit inside them, leaning against the walls with the help of his elbows and knees. The rest of the prisoners would sit outside. There was a narrow peephole in the metal door which the prisoners called "I-see-you-you-no-see-me." Suddenly I understood how awful it was to be transported like that, in a metal tumbler. And after all, that was sixteen years ago.

Branches scraped against the top of the metal roof of the van. We all lurched forward as the truck braked to a stop. We climbed outside into light. Beyond the trees the yellow walls of the morgue dissecting room could be seen. There was a bell to the right of the door. I rang it. The door was opened by a man in an oilskin apron. Altmyae pulled out some documents and said something in Estonian. The attendant gestured us to follow him.

"I'm not going," Bykover said. "I'll faint."

"Neither am I," Altmyae said. "I'll have nightmares afterwards."

"You've arranged this very nicely," I said. "You should have warned me beforehand."

"We were counting on you. You've got the guts to do it."

"I don't even know how to knot a tie."

"I'll teach you," Bykover said. "I'll teach you how to make a 'Cambridge lotus.' You'll train here and then perform it there."

"I would go," Altmyae said, "only I'm extremely impressionable. And in general I have no great love of the dead. How about you?"

"The dead are my passion!" I said.

"Pay attention and learn," Bykover said. "Follow along in reverse image. The thin part goes here, the wide part here. We turn it twice. We pull the tip through. And then we hold it here and slowly tighten it. Look, it's lovely, isn't it?"

"Not bad," I said.

"The advantage of the Cambridge lotus is that it's so easy to untie. You just pull on the tip and that's it."

"Ilves will be thrilled," Altmyae said.

"Did you understand how to do it?"

"More or less, yes," I said.

"Try it out."

Bykover eagerly offered his flabby neck, which was patched in four places with Band-Aids.

"Fine," I said. "I remember."

The inside of the morgue was cool and reverberant. Brown walls, cement, the Civil Defense instructions, a fire extinguisher colored a provocative scarlet.

"This one," the attendant indicated.

By the window, high on a calico-covered pedestal, stood the coffin. Not your commonplace brown, like the color of a safe, but black with foil lace.

Ilves looked absolutely dead. Lifeless as a plaster cast.

I showed the tie to the guard. As it happened, he spoke good Russian.

"I'll lift and you tie."

Locking his hands, he lifted the body as if it were a log. Then came the bumping and fumbling of our hands. "This way . . . a little more . . ." The collar sticking up, crumpled paper lace . . .

"*O kay*," the attendant said, smoothing the dead man's hair.

I took out the Journalists' Union pin and attached it to the dark blue serge lapel. The attendant brought the coffin lids with six bolts. We checked the fit and screwed the bolts in.

"I'll call my friends," I said.

THE COMPROMISE

Bykover and Altmyae came in. Fima's eyes were tightly shut. Altmyae smiled wanly. We carried out the coffin. It made a sickening squeak as we pushed it into the back of the van.

Altmyae climbed into the truck cab. Bykover was silent the whole way back. And just as we were pulling up, he said philosophically, "A man lived, lived, and then died."

"And what else did you expect?" I said.

People were milling about in the vestibule. They spoke in muted voices. Prints of a photo exhibit called "Youth of the Planet" glinted along the walls.

A man wearing an armband came out and announced loudly, "Smoking is permitted."

This small humane transgression satisfied the mourners.

The official organizers scurried noiselessly through the crowd. I didn't know any of them. Funeral rites evidently destroy the usual system of hierarchy. Out of those who volunteer to conduct the proceedings, nameless people seem to take over.

I approached an organizer. "We've brought the coffin."

"Have you got the cable too?"

"What cable? This is the first I've heard of it."

"Fine," he said, as if I had committed an insignificant blunder. Then he raised his voice, not losing the tone of deep sorrow: "Comrades, to the cars!"

Two women hurriedly and belatedly threw pine branches on the floor.

"It seems we're no longer needed," Altmyae said.

"I'm scheduled to speak."

"You speak at the end. In the beginning, the comrades from the Central Committee will give eulogies. And only afterwards the people who care to. All those who want to."

"What do you mean, 'all those who want to'? I'm scheduled. And the text has already been approved."

"Naturally. You're scheduled to want to speak. I saw the list. You're eighth. After Lembit. He wants everyone to sing. There's a song called 'Cranes.' 'It seems to me at times that the soldiers . . .' And so on. So Lembit's going to propose that everyone sing it."

"But who's going to sing? And out in this heat, no less."

"Everyone. Wait and see."

"You, for example, are you going to sing?"

"No," Altmyae said.

"And you?" I asked Bykover.

"If necessary, I'll sing," Fima answered.

People were shuffling toward the exit. Many carried wreaths, bouquets, or potted flowers. By the entrance of the building, six buses and our van stood waiting. The chief organizer walked over to me.

"Comrade Shablinsky?"

"He's on assignment."

"But you're from *Soviet Estonia*?"

"Yes. I've been scheduled—"

"Did you bring the body?"

"The three of us did."

"You'll accompany it for the rest of the time. You'll go in the special car. And here's something to keep up your courage."

He held out a package that made a sloshing sound. This was a veiled form of honorarium. A swallow before the attack. I became embarrassed but kept quiet. Stuck the package in my pocket. Told Bykover and Altmyae. We stopped by the snack bar and asked for glasses. Altmyae bought three sandwiches. The vestibule emptied. The pine branches contrasted darkly with the shiny yellow floor. We walked over to the van. The driver said, "There's room in the cab."

"That's all right," Altmyae said.

"Shall we give him 'a little one'?" I asked in a whisper.

"Not on your life," Bykover ordered sharply.

The coffin stood in its former place. For a little while we sat in the half-darkness. The motor started up. Altmyae set the sandwiches on the lid of the coffin. I got out the vodka. Fima tore off the tiny tin cap with his teeth. We touched glasses quietly. The van began to move.

"To his memory," Bykover said sadly.

Altmyae forgot himself and exclaimed, "This is good!"

We drank up, shoved the little bottle under the bench. The paper we threw out the window.

"We should bring the glasses back," I said.

"They'll still come in handy," Bykover remarked.

The van bumped over a crossing.

"We've reached our destination," Bykover said.

His voice had in it a note of life's impermanence.

The Linnamets Cemetery was spread out on hills which were overgrown with firs and strewn with impressive, moss-covered boulders. Looking at decorative rocks such as these, journalists like to say, "Remnants of the ice age." As if they themselves had survived from prehistoric times and remembered them well.

Everything here spoke of immortality and peace. The hills stood like the ruins of an ancient fortress. In the far distance an invisible sea rumbled. The crowns of the pine trees swayed. The bark on their yellowish parallel trunks was peeling.

No announcements, posters, kiosks, or garbage bins. A lake, monuments: water and stone in solemn alliance. Quiet.

We drove out onto the main cemetery avenue, striped by the shadows of pine trees. The driver braked. The metal door was flung open. Buses had lined up in a column behind us. The chief organizer walked over.

"How many of you are there?"

"Three."

"We'll need three more."

I understood that the coffin was still our problem.

People with wreaths and bouquets of flowers were crowding

near the buses. Suddenly, music began. The first powerful chord was followed by an echo. We were joined by three hefty fellows, freelance workers from the *Youth* newspaper. One I knew; we often played Ping-Pong together. We hoisted up the coffin. Then we turned around and took our place at the head of the column. Chopin's "Funeral March" was being played. To walk slowly with a heavy load is torture. I got tired. It was impossible to switch hands.

In a stifled voice, Bykover suddenly said, "He's heavy, the bastard . . ."

"Let's walk faster," I said.

We paced a little faster. The orchestra increased its tempo. Then still faster. We walked along, conducting. Bykover said, "I'm about to drop it."

Then louder, "Someone take over, comrades . . . Allo!"

He was replaced by a radio announcer named Oya.

At the end of the avenue was a dark, rectangular grave. Beside it a little mound of fresh earth had been heaped. The musicians spread out in a half-circle. At a pause in the music we lowered the coffin. The mourners surrounded the grave. The chief organizer and his assistants took the lid off the coffin. I made sure that the tie was in place, and then walked off behind the trees. The cameramen from the television studio started setting up their equipment. The light of the high-intensity lamps seemed out of place. Black cables lay in the grass. Bykover and Altmyae came over to me. Obviously, we had been united by the vodka. We lit cigarettes. The organizer asked for silence. The first speaker, holding a brand-new velvet hat in his hand, began his eulogy. I didn't listen. Then others delivered their speeches. The boys from the television studio kept calling to each other cheerfully.

"Live coverage," Bykover said. Then he added, "I myself will be buried like a dog."

"The sanitation department won't allow it," Altmyae responded. "The road to death is paved with meaningless news briefs."

"They have a lot of meaning," Bykover said indignantly.

The next person called upon to speak was some important personage from the *Ichta Lecht* newspaper. I caught one phrase: "His father and grandfather fought against Estonian autocracy."

"Now what are they talking about?" Altmyae said, startled. "There was never an autocracy in Estonia."

"Well, against tsarism," Bykover said.

"And there was no Estonian tsarism either. There was Russian tsarism."

"Well, one thing is sure: there certainly was no Jewish tsarism," Bykover remarked. "If there wasn't, there wasn't."

An organizer came up to us. "Are you Shablinsky?"

"He's away on assignment."

"Ah, yes . . . Are you ready? You go on after this next speaker."

Altmyae got out his cigarettes. His lighter didn't work. The lighter fluid had run out. Bykover went off to get matches. In a moment he returned on tiptoe. Gesticulating, he said, "Now you're going to laugh. That isn't Ilves."

Altmyae dropped his cigarette.

"That is—how is that?" I asked.

"It's not Ilves. It's another man. I mean, another dead man."

"Fima, do you know what you're talking about?"

"I'm telling you, it's not Ilves. It doesn't even look like him. What do you think, I don't know Ilves?"

"Is it possible this is a provocation?" Altmyae said.

"Obviously you got him mixed up."

"It must have been the attendant who got him mixed up with somebody else," I said. "I never saw Ilves in person. We've got to do something."

"What next?" Bykover said. "What about the live broadcast?"

"But this is—God only knows what!"

"I'll go take a look," Altmyae said.

He went off, came back, and said, "It really isn't Ilves. But there is some similarity . . ."

"And what about his relatives and friends?" I asked.

"Basically, Ilves didn't have relatives or friends," Altmyae said. "To put it bluntly, he wasn't too well loved."

"But they say he had a son, a nephew . . ."

"Put yourself in their place. A live TV broadcast is under way. And quite an important occasion."

People by the grave began to sing. You could pick out the piercing descant of Luba Torshina from the Human-Interest Department of our newspaper. Then the chief organizer nodded at me. I walked to the grave. Finally the singing died down.

"The final words will come from . . ."

Of course he garbled my name: "The final words will come from Comrade Dolmatov."

What haven't I been called in my life? Dokladov, Zaplatov . . .

I stepped up to the grave. Inside it, water had puddled and the stumps of cut roots showed white. Beside the grave, on special trestles, the coffin stood raised, and cast a shadow. The unknown man was covered with flowers. The small patch of his face, looking orphaned, was lost in the white foam of orchids and gladioli. Deprived of a name, the dead man seemed like an object. I saw the cupola of the blue tent propped up by pine trees. Jackdaws flew by, as they do on a television screen. The blindingly yellow spire of the church which towered above the houses of nearby Mustamyae brought out their dreary, everyday grayness. The grave was surrounded by strangers in dark coats. I could smell the stifling odor of flowers and pine needles. The edges of the uncomfortable bed pressed against my shoulders. The fallen petals tickled my hands crossed on my chest. Above my head a

TV cameraman was fussing with something. A faraway voice sounded, colored by self-admiration:

"I didn't know this man: his soul, his impulses, his determination, courage, disappointments and hopes. I don't believe that he found the truth without a search. I don't think that his departing glance discovered the full measure of life's turmoil, the all-too-obvious acts of cunning, the victories without triumphs, and the capitulations without bitterness. I don't think that he understood where we are going or what in our spasmodic retreat is joyful and valuable. And nevertheless, he is here . . . by his own choice . . ."

I heard a quiet, growing murmur. From the muffled phrases I could make out, "What's he saying?" Someone touched my sleeve. I moved my shoulder. I began to talk faster:

"What am I thinking of, standing beside this grave? Of the mysteries of the human soul. Of overcoming death and spiritual grief. Of the laws of existence born in the depths of millennia which will live till the extinction of the sun . . ."

Someone led me to one side.

"I don't understand," Altmyae said. "What did you have in mind?"

"I don't understand it myself," I said. "There was a kind of chaos all around me."

"I just found out everything," Bykover said. His face was lit with the slyness of someone initiated into a mystery. "He's the accountant of a fishing collective, and his name is Gaspel. At this moment Ilves is being buried as Gaspel at the Merival Cemetery. There's an unbelievable scene going on there. They just called. The family is in hysterics. It's been decided to go ahead with the burial as it is."

"Tomorrow or even tonight they can just switch the tombstones," Altmyae said.

"Out of the question," Bykover objected. "Ilves was a nomenclatured person. He has to be buried in a cemetery for the privileged. An ironclad order must be observed. At night they'll switch the coffins."

I suddenly lost my sense of reality. In the world revealed to me, there were no perspectives. The future crowded behind my back. The past hid the horizon. I began to feel that harmony had been invented by poets in their desire to touch the hearts of human beings.

"Let's go," Bykover said. "We'll get seats on a bus. Otherwise, we'll have to shake in that metal box all the way back."

THE NINTH COMPROMISE

("Soviet Estonia." July 1976.)
THE HARDEST DISTANCE. Tina Karu comes from a close-knit family, graduated school with a gold medal, served as Secretary of the Komsomol Committee, was always keen on sports. Here one characteristic detail about her has to be stressed. Of the various forms of "light" sports, she preferred the four-hundred-meter sprint; and this distance, according to specialists, is the most labor-consuming, demanding a combination of speed, endurance, explosive force, and an intense will to win. Stubborn determination, consistency and rigor, an ascetic way of living—these are the factors which have determined the course of Tina's life story and the path to her chosen goal. After finishing school, Tina entered the Department of Chemistry of Tartu University, took part in the activities of the Student Scientific Society, and gladly carried out her duties as a Komsomol. In her last year there, she became a member of the Communist Party. She then went on to become a graduate student at the Institute of Chemistry of the Academy of Sciences of the Estonian Republic. As a specialist in chemistry, Tina is interested in the mechanism of how carcinogenic substances act on man's organism. Her dissertation is close to completion.

Tina Karu sets high, realistic goals for herself. You can believe that she will attain success, going her own hard distance.

I met Tina Karu through friends we had in common. An interesting, quite intelligent woman—a young scientist. I wrote a little character sketch about her for the paper. From time to time I'd run into her at various scientific functions. Then one time she called me up. "Are you free? I have to talk to you about something."

I came to the Cafe Raya. Ordered some gin. She said, "I've been married for four years. Up to now, everything's been all right. Then last summer Rudi went to Moscow. When he came back, it all started."

"?"

"Something strange is going on. He wants . . . How can I explain this to you? We've become strangers . . ."

I forced myself to ask bluntly, "In sexual matters?"

"That's it."

"In what way, then, can I help?"

"You mean, why have I turned to you? You're the only amoral man I know. So I want to have a consultation."

"I don't understand."

"To discuss the situation."

"Well, I really don't discuss these matters, even with men. But a friend of mine has a book called *The Technology of Sex*. I can borrow it, if you want. Only not for long. It's his bedside book. Do you read Russian easily?"

"Of course."

I brought her *The Technology*. It's a wonderful book. You open to the first page, to the word "Introduction," and it's funny already. One of the sections begins, "For lovers with overly large stomachs, we recommend Position #7." The compassionate author even gives attention to such despised beings as pot-bellied lovers.

I gave her the book. She brought it back a week later.

"Did you understand everything?"

"Everything except one word: 'languorously.' "

I explained what that meant.

"Now I would like to test its practical application."

"I bless you, my daughter!"

"Only, not with my husband. I need some training first."

I have to emphasize that all this was said without a trace of flirtatiousness, and in the Estonian manner—down-to-earth and businesslike.

"Are you an amoral man?" she asked.

"Not entirely."

"Does that mean you refuse?"

"Tina," I begged, "this is not the way these things are done! We have a good comradely relationship. Given time, perhaps, it might change into other feelings . . ."

"How much?"

"What do you mean—how much?"

"How much time?"

"Oh Lord, I don't know . . . A month, two months . . ."

"No good. I have to take comprehensive examinations in April. Introduce me to someone. Preferably dark-haired. Surely you have some low-life friends?"

"Almost exclusively," I said.

I sat and thought. Shablinsky, of course, is an ace, but crude. Rosenshtein is building his dacha and has no strength left. Gulyayev—is blond. Mitya Klensky has the clap. Oska Chernov? Maybe he's suitable. Shy, ardent, and dark. True, a little stingy, but that's all right. For one time it won't matter.

I asked Chernov, "Have you had a lot of women?"

"Thirty-six, and four that are questionable."

"What does that mean—'questionable'?"

Oska lowered his eyes. "Certain kinds of deviations."

He'll do, I thought. I put the heart of the matter to him. Oska was dumfounded.

"As it happens, I once saw her. I even thought she was attractive. But you must admit, to do it like this, in such a utilitarian way . . ."

"Then what's the difficulty?"

"All the same, I'm a man."

"So help out another person."

I bought a bottle of rum out of my own pocket and invited

Tina and Oska to my place. Tina whispered to me, "I've made an arrangement with my girlfriend. I can use her apartment for three hours."

We drank and listened to the BBC. Oska tried to start a philosophical conversation. "Yes, it's the persecuted organizations that really know how to hang on to life through everything—"

Tina interrupted him. "We have to go. Otherwise my friend might get back."

They set off. In the morning Tina phoned me.

"So, how was it?" I asked.

"He saw me to the door and left."

I called Chernov. "What's wrong with you? Don't you have a conscience?"

"Believe it or not, old man, I can't do it. Somehow it just doesn't work for me."

"What kind of a man are you, after this?"

Oska became indignant. "I've had more women than you've eaten chopped-meat patties. But I've never met one like her. The surprising thing is that I'm attracted to her."

I invited them both over again. Served the rum they didn't drink the first time. They left. Tina called. "To hell with this friend of yours!"

"Surely he didn't desert again?" I said.

"Well, we got into a taxi. Oska paid in the dark. Shoved a ten-ruble note at the driver instead of a one. When he realized this later, he got terribly upset. He walked home on foot. I saw him hand the driver the ten. I thought that was the custom in Georgia. That he wanted to impress me. All Georgians are big spenders. Oska is a Georgian, isn't he?"

"No, Oska's Jewish. His real name is Malkiel."

I called him once more. "Come on, Oska, be a man!"

"You see, I had a ten-ruble note, a one, and some change . . ."

For the third time I invited them to my apartment.

"Listen," I said. "Tonight I'm sleeping at the office. And you stay here. There's some schnapps in the refrigerator. If the telephone rings, don't worry about it. Shall I lock the door so Oska doesn't run away?"

"Don't worry, I'm not going to run away."

So I headed off to my job on the overnight desk at the newspaper. Later, Tina called me there. "Come downstairs for a moment."

I came down to the lobby. She took some chocolate and a bottle of Long John whiskey out of her briefcase.

"Come here," she said, "and let me kiss you. And don't be afraid—it's just between good comrades."

She kissed me. "If you only knew how grateful I am to you!"

"Thank Oska."

"I gave him back the ten rubles, the ones he gave the taxi driver."

"That's shameful."

"It's all right. He earned them honestly."

I put the bottle in my pocket and went back upstairs to finish an article on a moral subject.

THE TENTH COMPROMISE

("Soviet Estonia." August 1976.)
TO: MOSCOW. THE KREMLIN. L. I. BREZHNEV. TELEGRAM. Dear and Much-Respected Leonid Ilych! I want to share with you a happy event. In the past year I was able to attain unprecedented labor statistics. I milked out of one cow a record-breaking amount of milk.

And still another happy event has occurred in my life. The Communists of our farm together chose me to become a member!

I promise you, Leonid Ilych, to work henceforward with even greater enthusiasm.

Linda Peips.

TO: ESTONIAN SSR. PAIDA REGION. LINDA PEIPS. TELEGRAM. Dear Linda Peips! I and my comrades thank you from the bottom of our hearts for the successes you have attained. Self-sacrificing labor for the good of one's native land ennobles human life by the feeling of being part of the struggle for the attainment of Communist ideals.

Permit me as well to congratulate you from the heart on the occasion of an unforgettable event—your joining the ranks of the Communist Party. For the Party is the advance-guard of Soviet society, its glorious vanguard.

Leonid Brezhnev.

Chief Editor Turonok split the seat of his trousers. They split without noticeable strain or sound; rather, they parted along the seam. This could be viewed as a drawback of soft imported flannel.

Around noon, Turonok approached the counter of the company bar. The luminescent blueness of his editorial drawers was revealed to all his flunkies, who obsequiously let him pass without waiting on line.

The staff workers started exchanging looks . . .

I am telling this story in such detail for two reasons. The first is that any embarrassment to people in authority gives me great pleasure. Second, the split in Turonok's pants had a certain impact on my fate.

But to return to the episode at the counter.

. . . The staff workers started exchanging looks, some malicious, some compassionate. The malicious ones were sincere, the compassionate ones hypocritical. And here, as always, the head flunky showed up, unselfish and inspired. This type of flunky worships authority so much that he confuses the Boss with the Motherland, the epoch, the universe.

To make it short, enter Edik Vagin.

On any newspaper staff there is always someone who does not want to—cannot and should not—write. And hasn't for years. Everyone gets used to this, and no one wonders about it anymore. This is the more remarkable since journalists like Vagin are always exhausted and feverishly preoccupied. Our local wit, Shablinsky, calls this condition "vaginalism."

Vagin was always hurrying somewhere, always saying hello in an abrupt, nervous way. At first, I naïvely took him for an alcoholic. Among the infinite modes of hangover I've noted his particular variation: a kind of tormented flight from daylight, the vibrating agility of a fugitive overcome with pangs of conscience.

Later I learned that Vagin didn't drink. And if someone doesn't drink *and* doesn't work, that makes you wonder.

"A mysterious man," I said.

"Vagin's an informer," Bykover told me. "What's mysterious about it?"

Our offices were located on Pikk Street, exactly across from 1 Pagari Street, the KGB headquarters. Vagin would walk over every day, or almost every day. We would see him crossing the street from our windows.

"Vagin's getting overtime!" Shablinsky would yell down.

But I've gotten off the track again.

. . . The staff workers started exchanging looks. Vagin touched the editor's shoulder lightly.

"Boss, there's some disorder in your clothes."

And here the editor committed a blunder. He hastily went for his fly with both hands, and proceeded to do what musicians call a light run up the keyboard. Convinced himself that the frontiers were closed. He turned red and said, "Find a better application for your humor."

He turned around and walked out, flooding his subordinates with the neon radiance of his underwear.

Then a short and slightly mysterious dialogue took place.

Vagin was standing there looking disheartened when Shablinsky came up to him.

"What did you butt in for?" he said. "It's better as it is."

"Better for whom?" Vagin gave him a sidelong glance.

"For you, naturally."

"Why better for me?"

"The thing is—"

"No! Why better? Why better?" Vagin was shouting. "Let him say it!"

"And you go to hell," Shablinsky said after a short pause.

"You see!" the informer exclaimed triumphantly.

He was an ordinary, clumsy informer with no style.

I didn't have time to feel sorry for him, since I had just been called to the editor's office. I was slightly uneasy, having just prepared the material for a two-hundred-line story to be entitled "Papa Is Taller Than the Sun" about an exhibit of children's drawings. So what does he want, I'd like to know? And now this untimely tear in his pants on top of it all! Maybe the editor was thinking that I had arranged it. There had already been a situation like that. I'd been assigned to write a long piece on an exhibition

THE COMPROMISE

of show dogs, which I went to cover. The editor, a great animal lover, showed up in a state-commissioned car to have a look for himself. And just then a thunderstorm began. Turonok got upset and said to me, "It's impossible to count on you."

"What do you mean by that?"

"Always some unforeseen complications."

As if I were Zeus and had personally arranged a thunderstorm.

I entered his office. The editor was sauntering around between the plaster bust of Lenin and a stereo set.

Some sort of portrait of Lenin is absolutely required in every executive office. I know of only one exception, and even that one is only partial. I had a friend named Avdeyev, the executive secretary of a youth newspaper. His father was a provincial actor from Lugansk who for years played the role of Lenin in his theater. So Avdeyev rather cleverly managed to get out of this situation by hanging over his desk a huge photograph of his papa in the role of Vladimir Ilych. No one could complain: it does seem like Lenin, but all the same it's Papa.

Turonok kept pacing between the bust and the stereo. I checked to see that the tear was in place. If one can put it that way. If something embarrassing can have its proper place.

At last the editor began. "You know, Dovlatov, you know how to use a pen!"

I said nothing. I don't blush from praise.

"You have the ability to see, to notice. Let's be frank. The cultural level of Russian journalists in Estonia leaves much to be desired, so to speak. The tempos of ideological growth are outstripping—to a large extent, I would say—outstripping the pace of cultural development. Think of the last session of the factory managers' collective. Klensky didn't know what a synonym was. Tolstikov declared in his opening statement, 'The Communists of the factory in the next few months must liquidate this impermissible status quo.' Repetsky entitled the agricultural editorial 'Nuts for export!' How do you like that?"

"A little intimate."

"To make it short: You possess erudition, a sense of humor. You have an original style. What's missing is a certain inner organization, discipline. In general, it's time to get to work. To go forth, as they say, on the expanse of great journalism. There's a curious item here under consideration. From the Paida region they inform us that a certain Peips has produced a record-breaking amount of milk."

"Peips—is that a cow?"

"Peips is a dairymaid. Moreover, she is a deputy of the Soviet of the republic. The statistics she gives are record-breaking. It's either two hundred liters or two thousand. To make it short, a lot. You can find out exactly how much at the Regional Party Headquarters. We thought up the following operation. The dairymaid should send a report to Comrade Brezhnev. Comrade Brezhnev will answer her, as coordinated. The letter to Comrade Brezhnev will have to be composed, ceremonies will have to be attended, then all this reflected in the press."

"This should go to the agricultural department."

"You will go as a special correspondent. We can't entrust this kind of assignment to just anyone. Ordinary newspaper clichés would be inappropriate in this case. We need a human touch here, understand? In general, it's time to get going. Get yourself a travel requisition and God be with you. We'll send a telegram to the Regional Party Headquarters."

During the whole conversation I experienced a strange sensation. Something about the editor seemed to me not quite usual. Then I realized it was the matter of the tear in his pants, which somehow made us equals. It took away his executive eminence and put us on the same plane. I felt sure that we were alike: two middle-aged hacks in identical (here I have to disclose a small secret) blue underwear. For the first time I felt sympathy for Turonok. I said, "Henry Franzovich, your pants are torn in back."

Turonok calmly walked over to a huge mirror, bent over, made sure, and said, "*Golubchik*, do me a favor . . . I'll give you some thread. There's some in the safe. For friendship's sake, not out of duty. Just put a few stitches in. After all, I can't ask Plyukhina . . ."

Galya Plyukhina was the newspaper sex diva, with studied grace notes in her voice like an opera singer. And an idiotic habit of biting . . . Anyway, I'm getting off the track again.

. . . "After all, I can't ask Plyukhina, can I?" the editor said.

There it is, I thought, your subconscious.

"Do it, pal."

"You mean to say—sew it up?"

"As I said, just a few stitches."

"The fact is, I can't sew."

"Do it as well as you can."

To make it short, I sewed up his pants. After all, why make a big deal out of it?

I stopped by the photolab to see Zhbankov. "Get ready," I said. "We're going off."

"One moment," Zhbankov said, livening up. "I'm coming. Except all I have on me is forty kopecks. Zhora owes me seventy."

"I'm not talking about drinking. We've got a job."

"A *job*?" Zhbankov said.

"What? You don't need money?"

"I need it. I've only got four rubles left till payday."

"The editor's sending us on a three-day trip out of town."

"To where?"

"Paida."

"Oh, good! We can buy smoked fish."

"That's what I said, let's get going."

I called Turonok on the office phone. "Can I take Zhbankov with me?"

The editor thought about it. "You and Zhbankov make, to be frank, a dangerous combination." Then he must have remembered the favor I did him because he said, "You'll be responsible. And remember: this is a serious assignment."

And so I began moving up. Before this I had been like the Soviet ruble, which everyone likes and which can't fall. With the dollar it's different. It climbed to incredible heights, and now it's falling, falling.

The journey began in an unusual manner—namely, Zhbankov arrived at the station completely sober. I didn't even recognize him at first—wearing a suit, and looking so sad.

We found our seats and started smoking. "Good for you," I said. "You're in fine shape."

"You see, I decided to put on the brakes a little. There's the danger of a full-scale crack-up. I have to think of the family, the children. The oldest is already four years old. Lera went to his kindergarten class and his teacher singled him out and praised him. Well developed mentally, she says. Sensible, energetic, already practicing onanism. Just like his daddy. He's such a little mite, you understand, and already he can figure things out."

Above Zhbankov's head, in his briefcase, something clinked. The train had begun to move.

"What do you think," Zhbankov asked. "Is the snack bar open?"

"You've got stuff with you."

"How do you know?"

"I just heard something clinking."

"Maybe those are developing chemicals?"

"Sure."

"Actually, of course, I do have booze with me. But think about it. We get there at six in the morning. Suppose we have to get over a hangover? What will we do then? Everything shut. A vacuum. A void in the wilderness."

"The local Party secretary will be there to meet us."

"What, with a half-bottle? How is he supposed to know what kind of people we are?"

"And who wanted to put on the brakes a little?"

"I did, for a time. But that was practically twenty-four hours ago. Practically an eon."

"The snack bar is open," I said.

We walked through several cars. It was quiet in the first-class coaches. Dun-colored carpets muted our footsteps. In the second-class cars we kept having to constantly apologize and step over bags and baskets of apples.

A few times, without special malice, people cursed at us. Zhbankov would say to them, "Expressing yourselves like that, by the way, is not necessary."

The carriage platforms droned from the cold wind. In the passageway between cars, as we pushed open the heavy doors with their low aluminum handles, the roar increased.

There were only a few people in the dining car. By the window sat two red-faced majors with their caps on the table. One was excitedly saying to the other, "Where's your calibrating line, Vitya? You've got to have a calibrating line. Because without a calibrating line, you yourself understand . . ."

His companion objected. "Was it a fact? It was. And a fact is a fact. Before a fact, as they say, that which . . ."

In the corner sat a Jewish family. A pretty, plump girl was wrapping a teaspoon in the corner of the tablecloth. A boy a little older kept looking at his watch. The mother and father spoke in barely audible voices.

We sat down at the counter. After a short silence, Zhbankov said, "Serge, explain something to me. Why do people hate Jews? Suppose they did crucify Christ. Of course they shouldn't have done it. But then so many years have gone by, and yet look . . . Jews, Jews. Vagin is Russian, Tolstikov is Russian, and they wouldn't have just crucified Christ, they would have eaten Him alive. That's where anti-Semitism should be directed, at Tolstikov and Vagin. Against people like them I feel this terrific anti-Semitism. How about you?"

"Naturally."

"If only they would launch an anti-Semitic campaign against Tolstikov! And all the Party hacks."

"Yes," I said, "not a bad idea. Only, don't shout."

"Speaking of which, take a look. Do you see those four people sitting there? Don't turn around. They look like they're sitting there so naturally, but something about them makes me mad. Our kind would sit in vomit. O kay! Those two meatheads get heated up over there. That's normal! But those four sit there so quiet, and somehow it burns me up. Maybe because they live well. If I was one of them I wouldn't live badly either, if only not for the lousy vodkaroo. Speaking of which, where is the service around here hiding itself?"

One major said to the other, "It's absolutely essential to have a scale of values, Vitya. A true scale of values. Plus a point of reference. For without a scale of values and a point of reference, as you can judge for yourself . . ."

The other objected as before. "It's a fact, Kolya! And a fact is a fact, no matter how you turn it around. A fact is a reality, Kolya! That is, something factual . . ."

The little girl dropped the teaspoon with a ringing sound. The parents scolded her quietly. The boy looked at his watch.

The snack bar attendant appeared—a woman with tight curls the color of floor polish. Behind her was a waiter with a tray, who served the Jewish family.

"Of course," Zhbankov said with annoyance. "Jews always have to be first."

Then he walked up to the counter. "A small bottle of vodka, naturally. And something lighter as a chaser."

We touched glasses and drank. From time to time the train braked and Zhbankov would hold on to the bottle. Then to a second.

At last he grew excited, turned pink, and became rather tiresome. "Old man," he yelled, "I work with a wide-angle lens. A wide-angle lens, you understand! I'm an artist by nature! And I have to shoot all kinds of nonsense—mugs that have no business being in front of a camera lens. I took a picture of one of them wearing about eight kilos of medals, all of them shining and glaring into the camera like the sun. And he's so pleased! Flatters me, you wouldn't believe! And all I get for it is six rubles, the official rate. Six rubles! They should go and try to get Raphael to paint the Mona Lisa for six rubles. I'm an artist . . ."

It was already past midnight. It was a struggle to get Zhbankov back to our compartment, and more of a struggle getting him to lie down. I handed him an aspirin tablet.

"Is this poison?" he asked, and then burst into tears.

I lay down and turned to the wall.

The conductor woke us ten minutes before our station. "You sleep, and we've already gone through Ikhiya Station," he said, displeased.

Zhbankov stared into space for a long time. Then he said, "When all the conductors get together, I bet one says to the other, 'I can forgive anything in a man. But if someone sleeps while we go through Ikhiya, I will always hold it against him.' "

"Get up," I said. "There will be people waiting for us there. Let's at least splash some water on our faces."

"Right now it would be nice to have something hot to eat," Zhbankov said dreamily.

I picked up a towel, got out a toothbrush and soap and a shaving razor.

"Where are you going?"

"To slaughter a sheep," I said. "You wanted something hot."

When I returned, Zhbankov was putting on his shoes. He launched a philosophical conversation—"So how much do you think we drank last night?"—but I interrupted him.

We were already pulling in. Beyond the window, the station landscape was framed in distinct lines. A pre-war building, flat windows, an illuminated clock.

We stepped out onto the platform. It was raw and dark.

"For some reason I don't hear trumpets," Zhbankov said.

But already someone was hurrying toward us—a tall man with a businesslike appearance, who was gesturing in a welcoming way.

"The comrades from the newspaper?" he asked with interest, smiling.

We gave our names.

"Please come this way."

By the outside lavatories a state-commissioned car was waiting. Beside it a thickset man in a raincoat was shifting from foot to foot.

"Regional Party Secretary Livak," he introduced himself.

The one who had met us turned out to be the chauffeur. Both spoke Russian almost without an accent. Most likely both had come from the Russified Estonian families who had settled near Leningrad long ago and now were always chosen for the top posts in Estonia.

"The first order of business is breakfast!" Livak announced.

Zhbankov perked up noticeably. "But everything's closed," he said coyly.

"Then we'll have to arrange something," the secretary said.

Small Estonian cities are cozy and hospitable. Paida in the early morning seemed as lifeless as a drawing. In the semidarkness, blue neon letters flickered.

"How was your trip?" Livak asked.

"Excellent."

"Are you tired?"

"Not at all."

"Fine. In any case you can rest up and have breakfast . . ."

We drove past the city center with its tuberculosis clinic and Party building. Then once again we were driving through the horizontal labyrinth of narrow suburban streets. Two or three sharp turns, and we were already on a highway. On the left was a forest, and on the right a flat shore and the shimmering smoothness of water.

"Where are we going to?" Zhbankov whispered. "Maybe they're taking us to a drying-out clinic?"

"We're almost there," Livak said. And as if he had guessed his thoughts: "We have here something on the order of a rest spa. With a restricted circle of guests. For our visitors."

"What did I tell you?" Zhbankov said, delighted.

The car stopped by a one-story building on the shore. White clapboard walls, a corrugated roof, a garage. Animating the picture, smoke rose lazily from the chimney. There were cement steps leading from the door to a little pier, and beside the mooring the white knifelike shape of a yacht jutted out.

"Well, here we are," Livak said. "Let me introduce you."

On the threshold stood a young woman of about thirty, in a canvas jacket and jeans. She had a lively, affable, slightly simian face, dark eyes, and strong even teeth.

"Bella Tkachenko," she introduced herself. "Second Secretary of the Regional Party Komsomols."

I gave my last name.

"Photojournalist Zhbankov, Mikhail," Zhbankov said softly, clicking his worn-down heels together.

"Bella Konstantinovna is your hostess," Livak said. "You'll relax here awhile. There are two bedrooms, a study, a sauna, a living room. You'll find sports equipment, a small library. Everything has been provided for. You'll see for yourselves."

Then he said something in Estonian. Bella nodded and called, "Evi! *Tule sinne!*"

Immediately, a blushing, very young girl in a T-shirt and shorts appeared. Her hands were blackened with ashes.

"Evi Sakson," Livak introduced her. "Correspondent of the *Regional Youth* newspaper."

Evi put her hands behind her back.

"I won't disturb you," Livak said, smiling. "All in all, the agenda goes like this. Rest up and have breakfast. I'll expect you at Party headquarters at three. I'll sign your travel-expense vouchers. You'll meet the heroine of the story. The material has to be ready by morning. And now excuse me, I have some business to attend to."

The Party secretary cheerfully ran down the steps of the porch. A moment later we heard the motor start.

There was an awkward pause. "Come in. Why are we standing here?" Bella said, suddenly remembering her duties.

We walked into the living room. Opposite the window a fire flickered in the fireplace, which was decorated with green tile. Deep armchairs stood in the corner.

They showed us to the bedroom. Two wide beds were covered with checkered camel's-hair blankets. On the night-table a massive crimson candle had been lit, illuminating the ceiling with a wavering rosy light.

"These are your quarters," Bella said. "In twenty minutes come have breakfast."

Zhbankov sat down carefully on one bed and for some reason took off his shoes. He began to talk with fear. "Serge, what have we got ourselves into?"

"What's wrong? We're simply moving up."

"In what sense?"

"We've been given a serious assignment."

"Did you get a look at those broads? Fantastic! I've never seen girls like that, not even in GUM! Which do you like better?"

"They're both fine."

"But maybe all this is a provocation? I mean, suppose you make a pass at her, and then *bam*, they haul you up in front of a judge."

"Why go right to 'bam'? We'll just relax, converse a little . . ."

"What is that—'converse'?"

" 'Converse' is when people talk to each other."

"Ah-h," said Zhbankov.

He suddenly crouched on his hands and knees and looked under the bed. Then for a long time he examined the electrical socket with mistrust.

"What are you doing?"

"I'm looking for a microphone. This is the natural place for a microphone. The listening device. A lush I know told me all about it."

"You'll find it later. It's time for breakfast."

We washed hastily. Zhbankov changed his shirt. "What do you think?" he said. "Should I bring out the half-bottle?"

"Don't be in such a rush," I said. "There's obviously some here. What's more, we've got to appear at Party headquarters today."

"I wasn't suggesting we get plastered. Just a little, for new acquaintance."

"Don't rush it," I said.

"And one more thing," he begged. "Don't start up one of your clever conversations. Sometimes you get going with Shablinsky, and then all I hear all evening is 'Avatar this, avatar that.' Think up something easier, like Sergei Esenin or Armenian radio jokes."

"Fine," I said. "Let's go."

The table was set in the living room. The standard assortment of Central Committee allocations: expensive cold-cuts, caviar, tuna, chocolate-covered marshmallows.

The girls had changed into bright-colored blouses and were now wearing fashionable shoes.

"Please take a seat," Bella said.

Evi picked up a tray. "Would you like a drink?"

"What else?" said my friend. "Anything else wouldn't be Christian."

Evi brought several bottles. "Cognac, gin and tonic, wine," Bella offered.

Zhbankov suddenly grew tense and said, "*Pardon*, I know that cognac. It's called KVN, or NKVD . . ."

"KVVK," Bella corrected him.

"Makes no difference. It costs sixteen-twenty a bottle. We're better off getting three bottles of vodka for that amount."

"Don't worry about it," Bella said.

And Evi asked, "Are you an alcoholic?"

"Yes," Zhbankov said clearly, "but within moderation."

I poured everyone some cognac. "To our meeting," I said.

"To our pleasant meeting," Bella added.

"Come on—down the hatch!" Zhbankov said.

We drank and fell silent except for the clatter of knives and forks.

"Tell us something interesting," Evi said.

Zhbankov lit a cigarette and began. "Life, girls, in essence, is like a kaleidoscope. Today it looks one way, tomorrow another. Today you get plastered, tomorrow one look and you kick the bucket. Remember, Serge, that disaster with the corpse?"

Bella leaned forward. "Tell us."

"The head of the TV studio died, a fellow named Ilves. Maybe he was the director, I don't remember. But he did die.

And in general he was right to do it. We hold a funeral for him, everything as it should be. The TV cameramen show up, the broadcast starts. There are speeches, naturally. Then the last farewell begins. I walk up to the coffin and look. It's not Ilves! How could I not know him? I must have photographed him a hundred times. But there in the coffin is some outside person."

"Alive?" Bella asked.

"Why alive? Naturally dead, as he should be. Only not Ilves. It turns out the corpses got mixed up in the morgue."

"How did it end up?" Bella asked.

"This is how. They buried the other guy. After all, you can't interrupt a live broadcast. But at night they switched the coffins. And anyway, what's the difference? It's the same business, only different—how can I put it—"

"Avatars," I prompted.

Zhbankov shook his fist at me.

"What a nightmare," Bella said.

"Stranger things have happened." Zhbankov was getting animated. "I'll tell you a story about somebody who hung himself. But first we'll have another drink."

I divided out the last of the cognac. Evi covered her glass with her palm. "I'm already drunk."

"No excuses," Zhbankov said.

The girls also lighted cigarettes. Zhbankov waited for silence and continued. "But the way he hung himself was pure comedy. This guy kept going on binges in the sleaziest way possible. His wife, naturally, nags him from morning to night. So he decides to hang himself. Not completely, just make-believe. In short—to give her a bad scare. His wife goes off to work. Just before she's due back, he attaches himself to the chandelier by his suspenders and hangs there. Then he hears steps, and he rolls up his eyes. For the effect, of course. But it turns out it's not his wife. It's one of their communal apartment-mates, a lady of about eighty, on business. She walks in, and there he is, hanging there."

"Horrible!" Bella said.

"The old lady turns out to be made of iron. No fainting. Instead, she goes up to him and starts fishing around in his pockets. And he's very ticklish, so he can't help giggling. Whereupon the lady signs off, once and for all. And he's hanging there and can't unattach himself. Now his wife comes in and takes in the scene: the old lady's dead and her husband's hung himself. So she goes to the telephone and dials. 'Vasya, something's happened. It's out of the *Arabian Nights*. But the result is, I'm free. Come over right away.' And her husband ups and says, 'I'll give it to that "come over." I'll poke his eye out, that fag!' and at that point his wife signs off too. Also for real."

"What a horror," said Bella.

"I can tell you more," Zhbankov said, "only, let's drink!"

"The sauna is ready," Evi said.

"What's that? We have to get undressed?" Zhbankov asked anxiously, adjusting his tie.

"Of course," Bella said.

We found ourselves in a dressing room. Exotic posters hung on the wall. The girls disappeared behind a screen.

"Well, Serge, our souls have ascended to paradise," Zhbankov muttered.

He undressed quickly, like a soldier, down to his ample satin drawers. On his chest was a blue tattoo: a bottle with a shotglass, a feminine profile, and an ace of hearts. And in the center, an inscription in ornamental Slavonic script: "Behold What Ruined Me!"

"Let's go," I said.

In the crowded sauna, which was made to look like a hut, it was unbearably hot. The thermometer read ninety degrees Centigrade. We had to pour cold water on the scorching planks.

The girls were wearing bright-colored, modern bathing suits, each divided into two narrow, disturbing strips.

"Do you know the rules?" Bella said, smiling. "You have to take off everything metallic. They could cause a burn."

"What things?" Zhbankov asked.

"Straight pins, safety pins, bobby-pins . . ."

"And teeth?"

"Teeth can be left in," Bella smiled. And she added, "Tell us another story."

"In a minute. Right now I'll tell you a story about how someone buried a wedding in liquid shit."

The girls went silent in alarm.

"A friend of mine used to drive a sanitation truck. Cleaned the stuff out of outhouses. And he has a girlfriend, very educated. 'The odor you give off,' she says, 'is not good.' And after all, what can he do about it? 'But then,' he says, 'the pay is good.' 'You could drive a cab,' she suggests to him. 'But do you know what the pay is like? A sparrow's navel.' A year goes by, and she finds herself another friend. Without odor. So she says to my pal, 'That's it. I don't love you anymore. The end.' He, of course, is all torn up. And for her and her friend it's wedding bells. They rent a public dining hall, there's drinking, carryings on . . . It gets dark. At that point my pal shows up in his shit-truck, *pardon*. Opens the transom, sticks his hose in, and opens his pump. And he's got about four tons of the stuff in the tank. Gets the guests up to their knees in it. Noise, screams—that's a send-off for you! The police arrive. The public dining hall has to be completely renovated. And my pal gets the automatic seven-year term. So there it is."

The girls sat there quiet and a little dispirited. I was suffering unbearably from the heat. Zhbankov was in a state of high bliss.

I began to have enough of all this. The alcohol was gradually evaporating. I noticed that Evi kept looking at me, maybe out of fear or maybe respect. Zhbankov was heatedly whispering something to Bella Konstantinovna.

"Have you been working for the newspaper long?" I asked.
"A long time," said Evi. "Four months."
"Do you like it?"
"Yes, very much."
"Where did you work before that?"
"I didn't work. I was in school."

She had a childish mouth and fluffy bangs. She spoke rapidly, earnestly, and a little breathlessly, with a crusty Estonian accent, sometimes mangling Russian words.

"What attracted you to newspaper work?"
"Why not?"
"But you have to lie so much."
"No, I do proofreading. I don't write yet myself. I wrote an article, and they said it wasn't good."
"What about?"
"Sex."
"What!"
"Sex. It's an important subject. There should be special magazines and books. People anyway make sex, only much is incorrect."
"And you know what is correct?"
"Yes. I gotten married."
"Then where's your husband?"
"He drowned. Drank some cognac and drowned. He was studying chemistry to Tartu."
"I'm sorry," I said.
"I've read much of your articles. There's a lot funny. And a lot of dots . . . nothing but dots. I'd like to work to Tallinn. The newspaper here is very small."
"All that lies ahead of you."
"I know what you said about the newspaper. Many people write not what really is. I don't like that way."
"And what do you like?"
"I like poetry, the Beatles . . . Should I say what else?"

"Go on."

"I like you too."

I thought I had misheard her. It was extremely unexpected. I hadn't known it was so easy to unnerve me.

"You're very handsome!"

"In what sense?"

"You look just like Omar Sharif."

"Who's that, Omar Sharif?"

"Sharif! He's the best!"

Zhbankov stood up unexpectedly. Pulled the door open. Awkwardly dashed down the cement steps to the river. For a second he froze. Waved his arms. Then uttered an unseemly animal-like howl as he fell in.

A fountain of waterspray rose up. From the depth of the disturbed river all sorts of jars, driftwood, and garbage floated up.

For about three seconds he disappeared. Then a black, unruly head surfaced, with the frantic eyes of a month-old puppy. Zhbankov, tottering, climbed up the shore. His thin loins were sculpturally draped in his long wet drawers.

After running around the cottage twice singing a popular film song, Zhbankov sat down on a sauna shelf and lighted a cigarette.

"So, how was it?" Bella asked.

"Normal," Zhbankov answered. And he loudly snapped the elastic of his drawers against his belly.

"How about you?" Bella said, turning to me.

"I prefer a shower."

There was a shower stall in the neighboring room. I took a shower and got dressed. "A silly seventeen-year-old provincial girl," I repeated to myself. "She drinks three glasses of cognac and goes crazy."

I went into the living room and poured myself a gin and tonic. From outside came the sound of shouts and splashing water.

Evi soon appeared, all pink, in a wet bathing suit. "Are you angry to me?"

"Not at all."

"I see . . . Wait, let me kiss you."

At this, I again became confused. Me, with all my experience. "You're starting up a bad game," I said.

"I'm not fooling you."

"But we're leaving tomorrow."

"You'll go here again."

I stepped toward her. Try staying reasonable yourself if there's a seventeen-year-old girl next to you who's just emerged from the sea. Or, to be more exact, from the river.

"What on earth are you doing? What's this?" I said.

"That's how Judy Garland always kisses," Evi said. "And she also goes like this . . ."

It's amazing how men are put together! Or am I the only one like this? You know it's all lying, primitive Party sham and lying with a Hollywood patina over it. You know it all but you're happy as a kid.

Evi had sharp shoulder blades and a backbone made of cold sea pebbles. She cried out softly and trembled. A fragile, many-colored butterfly in a loosely clenched fist.

At this point a deafening "*Pardon!*" was heard. Zhbankov loomed in the doorway. I let go of Evi.

He put a bottle of vodka on the table. He had evidently decided to release his reserves.

"It's already getting on toward one o'clock," I said. "They'll be waiting for us at Party headquarters."

"Aren't you conscientious," Zhbankov grinned.

Evi went to get dressed. Bella Konstantinovna also changed her clothes. She was now wearing a strict, drab, managerial suit.

And here I thought, if only there were no Party headquarters, no milk-crazed cow, if only I could live here without any serious assignments. The yacht, the river, the young ladies. Go ahead, let them lie, flirt, imitate cheap Hollywood stars. What a lovely thing they are, feminine affectations! Maybe I was meant to come into the world just for their sake! I'm thirty-four years old and have never had a single carefree day, lived a single day without worries, discontent, or longing. No, get ready to go to Party headquarters, where there are clocks, portraits, corridors, and everywhere an endless pretense of seriousness.

"Hey, folks! I just got my second wind!" Zhbankov announced.

I poured out the vodka—for myself, a full glass. Evi touched my sleeve. "Don't drink now. Later."

"Oh, this is all right."

"Livak is waiting for you."

"Everything will be fine."

"What do you mean, 'will be'?" Zhbankov said belligerently. "Everything is fine already! I've gotten my second wind! Come on, down the hatch!"

Bella switched on the radio. A low baritone was declaiming something painfully relevant to the moment:

There is no truth in this stormy world,
There's only an instant, but try to take hold of it.
There's only a flash between the past and the future,
Which is the thing that we call life!

We drank again and again. Evi sat on the floor beside my armchair. Zhbankov orated something, now and again leaving to go to the toilet. Each time he would say affectedly, "Would you ladies mind if I acquaint myself with the facilities?" And invariably he would add, "I've got to pour some off."

Suddenly I understood that I had gone past the point where I should have stopped. I felt a deceptive lightness and forced courage. The sensation of power and impunity grew.

"To hell with Party headquarters! Mishka, pour!"

Here Bella Konstantinovna took the initiative. "Boys, let's go and get it over with, and afterwards . . . I'll call for a taxi."

And she went to the telephone.

I stuck my head under the faucet. Evi pulled out a compact and said, "Don't see."

Twenty minutes later, our taxi pulled up to the Party building. All the way there Zhbankov had sung:

> *I don't want to talk to you,*
> *Don't yak nonsense, Manya.*
> *Better to go drink with the boys.*
> *Ech, the boys have real business on their minds.*

No doubt the mysterious Manya was the personification of Party headquarters and their various spheres.

Evi kept stroking my hand and whispering in a tone of disturbing indecency. Bella Konstantinovna looked severe.

She led us through the broad corridors. Everyone kept greeting her.

On the first floor loomed a tall bronze statue of Lenin. On the second, also a bronze Lenin, only smaller. On the third, Karl Marx with a beard like a funeral wreath.

"Interesting. I wonder who'll be monitoring the fourth?" Zhbankov said, smirking.

It turned out to be Lenin again, only this time made of plaster.

"Wait here a moment," Bella Konstantinovna said.

We sat down. Zhbankov sank into a deep armchair. His feet, in cheap, worn-out shoes, reached to the center of the reception room. Evi moderated her passion slightly. Her love calls were too much out of keeping with the propaganda posters.

Bella opened the door to us. "Come in."

Livak was talking on the telephone. His free hand welcomed us in encouragingly.

Finally he hung up. "Do you feel rested?"

"Personally, I certainly do," Zhbankov said weightily. "I've got my second wind."

"That's fine. Now you'll drive out to the farm."

"What on earth for?" Zhbankov exclaimed. "Oh, yes."

"Here are the facts concerning Linda Peips. The labor statistics, a short biography, citations of excellence. Where are your travel-expense vouchers? Stamp them here at the bottom. Now, if your evening is free, we can go somewhere. The performances at the drama theater are in Estonian, it's true. But there's the Rest and Recreation Park. The Intourist bar is open till one a.m. Bella Konstantinovna, organize a little excursion for the comrades."

"Can I speak freely?" Zhbankov raised his hand.

"Please do." Livak nodded to him.

"We're all friends here, right?"

"But of course."

"So I'll spill it out, just like in the Navy."

"I'm listening."

Zhbankov took a step forward and lowered his voice conspiratorially. "How about translating all this into kegs?"

"What do you mean?" Livak didn't understand.

"We should, I say . . ."

Livak looked at me in confusion. I pulled Zhbankov by the sleeve. He stepped to the side and continued. "In the sense of the nth degree of vodkaroo instead of the drama theater! Of course I madly beg your pardon . . ."

Astounded, Livak turned to Bella. She sharply enunciated, "Comrade Zhbankov and Comrade Dovlatov have been provided with everything necessary."

"Much wine," Evi added naïvely.

"What do you mean, 'much'?" Zhbankov objected. " 'Much' is a relative concept."

"Bella Konstantinovna, take care of it," the secretary ordered.

"That's the Navy way." Zhbankov cheered up. "That's how we do it."

I decided to step in. "Everything's clear," I said. "I have the information. Comrade Zhbankov will take the photos. The material will be ready by ten in the morning."

"Remember, the letter must be personal."

I nodded.

"But at the same time, the whole country will read it."

I nodded again.

"It's got to be a report . . ."

I nodded a third time.

". . . but a report to her nearest and dearest."

Another nod. Livak stood near me. I was afraid I would breathe alcoholic vapors on him. I think I did, anyway.

"And don't get carried away, comrades," he warned. "Don't get carried away. This is a very serious business. Everything in moderation."

"Want me to immortalize you and Dovlatov?" Zhbankov suddenly proposed. "You're both colorful-looking types."

"If possible, next time," Livak answered with impatience. "After all, we'll see each other again tomorrow."

"Fine," said Zhbankov. "Then I can take a shot in more decent surroundings."

Livak kept silent.

Downstairs a car was waiting with the same driver who had met us that morning. "We'll drop in for a short time at the farm, and that will be it," Bella said.

"Is it far?" I asked.

"About ten minutes away," the driver answered. "Everything is close here."

"It would be nice to get some refreshments on the way," Zhbankov whispered. "The fuel tank's nearly empty." Then he said to the driver, "Chief, pull up at the first food store. You won't tell on us, will you?"

"Why should I care?" The driver seemed offended. "I took off yesterday myself."

"Maybe you'll join us?"

"These are my work hours. Dinner's waiting at home."

"Fine, you know best. Would you have a utensil with you?"

"What do you think!"

The car stopped beside a local food store. There was a crowd by the counter. Zhbankov, holding up six rubles in his hand, energetically cleared a path. "I'm late for my plane, fellas. The taxi's waiting, you understand . . . The kid's sick . . . My wife, the bitch, is in labor." A minute later he emerged with two bottles of local brew.

The driver held out a cloudy glass to him.

"Well, here's to everything going *o kay*!"

"Pour some for me," I said. "What the hell."

"And who will do the photographs?" Evi said.

"Mishka will do everything. He's a good worker."

And in fact Zhbankov did excellent work, no matter how much he drank. Even though his equipment was the most primitive. Photojournalists were usually issued Japanese cameras which could cost as much as five thousand rubles. Zhbankov had not been issued one—"He'll sell it for booze," the editor had decided. Zhbankov took pictures with an ordinary Soviet camera worth nine rubles. He carried it in his pocket (the case had been lost). He used the same developer for weeks. There were always cigarette butts floating in it. The photographs, though, came out very clear, unstudied, with the sharp contrasts necessary for newspaper prints. Obviously, he had a special talent.

Finally, we pulled up to an administration building hung

with bulletin boards. Over the gates there was a red banner stenciled with the slogan, "Bone is a Valuable Industrial Raw Material." A few people stood in a group on the porch. The driver asked them something in Estonian, and they showed us the way.

The cowshed was a low, rather depressing building. Above the entranceway a dusty bulb burned, illuminating the befouled steps.

Bella Konstantinovna, Zhbankov, and I got out of the car. The driver smoked. Evi dozed in the back seat.

Suddenly a lame man appeared, carrying a leather briefcase. "Chief Agronomist Savkin," he introduced himself. "Come in."

We entered. Behind the plank partitions, cows could be heard stamping. Cowbells clanged, we heard heavy sighs and the rustle of hay. Lethargic animals looked us over languorously.

There's something pathetic about a cow—something abject and repulsive about her inability to refuse, her gluttony and indifference. This, despite her size and horns. An ordinary hen looks more independent. But a cow is a suitcase packed with beef and bran. (Actually, I don't know anything about them.)

"Come in, come in."

We found ourselves in a crowded little room which smelled of sour milk and manure. The table was covered with blue oilcloth. A lamp hung from a twisted cord. Along the walls were yellow plywood boxes for clothing. In the corner a milking machine glinted dimly.

A middle-aged woman in a green sweater rose to greet us. Medals and memorial pins glittered on her sloping chest.

"Linda Peips," Savkin announced.

We shook hands.

"I'm going," said the chief agronomist. "If you need something, call two-two-six on the local phone."

With some difficulty we all found places to sit. Zhbankov took his camera out of his pocket.

Linda Peips seemed a little nervous.

"She only speaks Estonian," Bella said.

"It's not important."

"I'll translate."

"Ask her something to make an impression," Zhbankov whispered to me.

"Ask her yourself," I said.

Zhbankov turned to Linda Peips and asked gloomily, "What time is it?"

"Translate this," I said, cutting him off. "How did Linda manage such high results?"

Bella translated. The dairymaid fearfully whispered something back.

"Write this down," Bella said. "The Communist Party and its Lenin Central Committee—"

"Got it," I said. "Could you find out if she belongs to the Party?"

"She belongs," Bella answered.

"For how long?"

"Since yesterday."

"One moment," Zhbankov said, aiming his camera. Linda froze, her eyes fixed in space.

"Everything's in order," Zhbankov said. "Six rubles in the bag."

"And the cow?" Bella asked in surprise.

"What cow?"

"In my opinion they should be photographed together."

"You couldn't fit a cow in here," Zhbankov explained. "And in there the lighting is lousy."

"So what are we going to do?"

Zhbankov shoved his camera back into his pocket. "There's a ton of cows back at the office," he said.

"What do you mean?" Bella said, surprised.

"I mean, in the archives there are all the cows you could want. I'll cut out your Linda and paste her on."

I touched Bella's sleeve. "Could you find out if she has a big family?"

She said something in Estonian. In a moment she translated. "The family is a big one. She has three children. Her oldest daughter is finishing high school, and the youngest son is only four."

"And her husband?" I asked.

Bella lowered her voice. "Don't write this down. The husband has left them."

"One of our kind!" Zhbankov said, cheered for some reason.

"Fine," I said. "Let's go."

We made our farewells. Linda looked after us with a slightly disappointed expression. Her carefully set hairdo shone from hairspray.

We walked out onto the road. The driver had managed to make a U-turn. Evi, wearing a suede jacket, was standing by the front of the car.

Zhbankov suddenly went slightly insane.

"*Kiik*," he yelled in Estonian. "That's it! We're done! Forward, comrades! On to new frontiers! To new attainments!"

In half an hour we were sitting by the river. The driver said goodbye in a restrained manner and left. Bella Konstantinovna signed his assignment papers.

The evening was warm and clear. Beyond the river the dimming edge of the sky had turned crimson. On the water, rose-colored patches of light trembled.

No one wanted to go in. We walked down to the pier, and for a while we were all silent. Then Evi asked me, "Why did you come to Estonia?"

How could I answer? By explaining that I had no home, no country or refuge? That I've always been searching for this quiet harbor? Or that I only ask one thing out of life—to sit like this, quiet and without thinking?

"The food supply," I said, "is good here. Night bars . . ."

"And you?" Bella turned to Zhbankov.

"I fought here," Zhbankov said, "and ended up staying. In a word, one of the occupying forces."

"How old are you anyway?"

"Not so old, forty-five. I caught the very end of the war when I was still a kid. I served as an orderly for Lieutenant Ader, and then was wounded."

"Tell us," Bella asked. "You tell stories so well."

"What's there to tell? I got hit with a piece of shrapnel. That's the whole love story. So, shall we go in?"

Inside the house the telephone began ringing. "Just a minute," Bella exclaimed, getting out her keys as she ran.

She came back quickly. "Yukhan Oscarovich wants to talk to you."

"Who?" I asked.

"Livak."

We went into the house. The light switch snapped and the windows went dark. I lifted the receiver.

"We've received an answer," Livak said.

"From whom?" I didn't understand.

"From Comrade Brezhnev."

"Uh—how is that? Your letter hasn't been sent yet."

"Well, what of it? It just means that Brezhnev's staff is a little more efficient than you . . . than us," Livak corrected himself tactfully.

"So what does Comrade Brezhnev write?"

"He sends his congratulations, his thanks for the successes attained, his wishes for personal happiness . . ."

"What now?" I asked. "Do I write the report or not?"

"You have to. That's the document, after all. I just hope

Comrade Brezhnev's office will backdate it."

"Everything will be done by morning."

"I'll be waiting."

The girls were busy reviving the leftovers. Zhbankov and I sat down together in the bedroom.

"Misha," I said, "don't you have the feeling that all this is happening to someone else? That it's not you, and not me? That it's some kind of idiotic play and we're just spectators?"

"Here's what I'm going to tell you," Zhbankov said. "Don't think. Just don't think, and that's it. I haven't thought for about fifteen years. Because if you think, you get depressed. Everyone who thinks is unhappy."

"And you, are you happy?"

"Me? At this very moment I'm ready to put my neck in the noose! Only I'm afraid of pain at the last minute. If only one could fall asleep and not wake up."

"So what can we do, then?"

"Don't think. Drink vodka."

Zhbankov got out a bottle.

"It seems I'm about to have a drink," I said.

"Why not?" Zhbankov winked. "Want a slug from the bottle?"

"But there's a glass here."

"The pleasure's not the same."

We each took a drink. There was nothing to eat with it. With pleasure I felt the alcohol start to work. The contours of life became less distinct and sharp.

Reporting the events that followed requires a certain amount of concentration.

I remember the rehabilitation of the scarcity-item Party delicacies. However, some squash and tomato stew, called "caviar," also made its appearance as an indicator of the general decline. Even the drink declined in quality from Mishka's hoarded bottle to some Yugoslavian slivovitz to the cheap local vodka.

After the tenth round, Zhbankov rose menacingly and started shouting, "I'm an artist! I photographed Khrushchev's wife! Even Giscard, the cunt, d'Estaing! I've had an exhibit in the House of Invalids! And you talk about a cow!"

"Dummy, my little dummy," Bella cooed to him. "Let's go, pussycat, and I'll put you to bed . . ."

"You're very sad," Evi said to me. "Something's wrong?"

"Everything," I said, "is terrific! A normal dog's life!"

"You shouldn't think so much. To be glad is the good thing to be."

"That's just what Mishka said too—drink!"

"Drink you've had enough. Now we'll go, I will be pleasing you."

"Which won't be hard," I said.

"You're very handsome."

"That's an old song, but how good it sounds!"

I poured myself a full glass. After all, I had to finish off this idiotic day somehow. And how many more of them lay ahead?

Evi sat on the floor beside my chair. "You don't resemble others," she said. "You have a good career, you're handsome. Only you're often sad. Why?"

"Because there's only this life and there won't be another."

"Don't think. Sometimes is better to be stupid."

"It's a little late for that," I said. "Better to drink."

"Only don't be sad."

"That's all over. I'm moving up. I've received a serious assignment. I'm stepping out onto the expanse of great journalism."

"Do you have a car?"

"Better ask me if I own a pair of socks with no holes."

"I want a car so much."

"You'll have it. I'll get rich and we'll buy one."

I drank and poured another glass. Bella was dragging Zhbankov to the bedroom. His legs dangled behind like two drooping gladioli.

"We too should go," Evi said. "You're already falling asleep."

"In a minute." I drank and poured again.

"Let's go."

"Look, I'm leaving tomorrow. And then you'll find some guy with a car."

Evi became thoughtful and laid her head on my knee. "When I marriage again, it will only be with a Jew," she announced.

"Why is that? Do you think all Jews are rich?"

"I'll explain it to you. Jews get circumcised."

"Well."

"Others don't."

"The swine!"

"Don't laugh. It's an important problem. When there's no circumcision, you can get smegma."

"What?"

"Smegma. It's a bad substance, a carcinogen. Down there. Want me to show you?"

"No, no. Better just tell me about it."

"With circumcision you don't get smegma. Then you don't get cervix cancer. You know what cervix is?"

"Well, let's say I have a general idea."

"The statistics show with no circumcision there's more cervix cancer. And in Israel it doesn't exist."

"What doesn't?"

"The cervix . . . the cancer of it. They have throat cancer, stomach cancer . . ."

"Also no joy," I said.

"Of course," Evi agreed.

We were silent. "Let's go," she said. "You're falling asleep."

"Wait. I have to get circumcised." I drank down a full glass and poured another.

"You're very drunk. Let's go."

"I have to get circumcised. Or even better, cut off the cervix and to hell with it!"

"You're very drunk. And angry to me."

"I'm not angry. We belong to two different generations. My generation is garbage, and yours is something fantastical."

"Why are you angry?"

"Because there's only this life. The minute has passed, and it's over and won't come again."

"It's already one in the morning," Evi said.

I drank and poured again. And at that very instant I felt as though I'd fallen through something. Suddenly I felt as though I were on the bottom of an aquarium. Everything swayed, swam away, there were glittering patches of light. And then everything disappeared.

. . . I woke to the sound of knocking. Zhbankov walked in. He was wearing a sports robe.

I was lying crosswise on the bed. Zhbankov sat down next to me.

"Well, how is it?" he asked.

"Don't ask."

"When I'm an old man," Zhbankov said, "I'll write a testament to my grandchildren and great-grandchildren. Or rather, an instruction. One single sentence. Do you want to hear it?"

"Well?"

"One sentence: 'Don't try to make love with a hangover.' Followed by three exclamation points."

"I feel awful. Completely awful."

"And there's nothing left for a cure. You swilled it all up."

"And where are our ladies?"

"Making breakfast. You have to get up. Livak's waiting."

Zhbankov went to get dressed. I stuck my head under the faucet. Then I sat down at the typewriter. In five minutes the text was ready.

"Dear and Much-Respected Leonid Ilych! I want to share with you a happy event. In the past year I was able to attain unprecedented labor statistics. I milked out of one cow . . ." ("Out of one cow" I wrote intentionally. In this turn of phrase you could hear living verisimilitude and touching peasant naïveté.)

The end went like this: "And still another happy event has occurred in my life. The Communists of our farm together chose me to become a member." Here the style was already limping visibly, but I had no strength to revise it.

"Breakfast," Bella called.

Evi was slicing bread. I wished her good morning guiltily. In response I got a smile like a rainbow and a sincere question: "How do you feel?"

"Couldn't be worse," I said.

Zhbankov was conscientiously investigating all the empty bottles. "Not a gram," he declared.

"Drink some coffee," Bella urged. "In a minute the taxi will be here."

I drank the coffee and felt no better. Food was out of the question.

"Some coins are still jumping around," Zhbankov said, pulling the change out of his pocket. Then he looked at Bella Konstantinovna. "Mother, would you throw in a ruble and a half?"

She took out her purse. "I'll send it to you from Tallinn," Zhbankov said.

"Never mind, you've earned it." Bella grinned cynically.

A car horn honked.

We collected our briefcases and got into the taxi. Soon Livak was shaking our hands. He approved my text without revision. What's more, he made a little speech.

"I am pleased, comrades. You have labored quite well and relaxed in a civilized manner. I'm glad to have made your acquaintance. For a Party worker and a journalist are, in a sense, colleagues, I would say. I wish you success on the difficult ideological front. Are there any questions?"

"Where's the snack bar around here?" Zhbankov asked. "We're in need of a wee cure."

Livak frowned. "Excuse me for using a crude Russian expression," he said, and he paused reproachfully, "but you're behaving like children!"

"What, not even any beer?" Zhbankov asked.

"You could be seen." Livak lowered his voice. "There are all kinds of people here. You know how it is at Party headquarters."

"Nice kind of work you chose for yourself," Zhbankov said, with some sympathy.

"By education I'm an engineer," Livak said unexpectedly.

Everyone was silent. Then the farewells began. Livak was already shuffling papers. "The car is waiting," he said. "I'll call the station. Go to Ticket Window Four and give my name."

"*Ciao!*" said Zhbankov, waving his hand.

We went downstairs and got into the car. The bronze Lenin watched us go. The girls came with us to see us off.

On the platform, Zhbankov and Bella went off to one side.

"Will you go here again?" Evi asked.

"Of course."

"And I will go to Tallinn. I'll call the newspaper office. So your wife won't be angry."

"I have no wife," I said. "Goodbye, Evi. Please don't be angry."

"Don't drink so much," Evi said.

I nodded.

"Because then you can't make sex."

I moved to her and put my arms around her and kissed her. Bella and Zhbankov were coming up to us. From his gestures it was obvious that he was lying outrageously.

We climbed into the compartment. The girls walked back to the car, talking with animation. They didn't even look back.

"In Tallinn we'll get rid of our hangovers," Zhbankov said. "I still have close to six rubles. And would you like to hear something really nice?" He winked at me. A joyful, triumphant smile lit up his face. "Zhora still owes me seventy kopecks!"

THE ELEVENTH COMPROMISE

("Soviet Estonia." October 1976.)
MEMORY IS A FORMIDABLE WEAPON! Greek mythology has given us the image of Lethe, the river of forgetfulness, whose waters carry away the earthly sufferings endured by human beings. On the shore of Lethe, man experiences a pitiful, momentary illusion of happiness. His naïve intellect, devoid of recollection, makes him a toy in the hands of fate. But from time immemorial, another current has flowed against Lethe's—the abundant and inexhaustible river of human memory.

In the city of Tartu, the Third All-Republic Reunion of Former Prisoners of Fascist Concentration Camps has opened.

Their faces are at the same time festive and severe. Each one wears a modest little memorial pin on his chest: a red triangle and the silhouette of a dove—the indissoluble emblems of spilled blood and peace. They gather in groups in the spacious halls of the Vanemuine Theater. There are greetings, embraces, excited conversations...

Lazar Borisovich Slapak, a construction engineer, tells us: "At first, I was sent to a camp for prisoners of war. Then I was transferred to Stutthof for spreading anti-fascist propaganda and for organizing escapes. We always could recognize our own kind by the eyes, by a gesture of the hand, by an elusive smile... A person doesn't feel that he's a victim if there are comrades and brothers around him."

The reunion will go on for two days. Two days of reminiscence, friendship, and loyalty to what has been lived through. The delegates and guests will then disperse, having replenished the precious and eternal archive of human memory. And we, following their lead, solemnly and sternly utter as a warning, as an oath and precept for the entire world: "No one is forgotten, and nothing is forgotten!"

We arrived in Tartu early in the morning. During the whole trip there Zhbankov had been busy repairing his camera. This operation consumed several paperclips, insulating tape, a small splinter of mirror . . .

At first, they had wanted to send Malkiel, but Zhbankov staged a protest. "Don't forget, I was a combat soldier. Where's your conscience?"

Editor Turonok tried to resist argument. "It's a gathering of former prisoners there, and not combat soldiers at all."

"As if I hadn't been a prisoner!" Zhbankov raised his voice.

"The drying-out clinic doesn't count," the editor said sarcastically.

But Zhbankov wouldn't back down. He had in reserve certain effective measures. If Misha was openly denied something, he started hinting that he would get drunk. He never said this directly. He would just ask, "So, is the mutual credit union still open?"

This signified that Misha intended to raise some cash. And if this wasn't possible, he'd hock the office photo-enlarger and drink up the proceeds.

As a rule, they gave in to him. This didn't stop Zhbankov from getting drunk regularly. The mere thought of heavy drinking was usually a sign that he was about to show up.

"Henry Franzovich," I said, butting in, "Zhbankov and I have already gone on assignment together."

"We have a mutual creative understanding," Misha seconded.

"That's just what frightens me," Turonok said. "And also, by the way—well, fine. Go."

I think that the editor must have remembered that this was an important assignment. And Misha really was a superb photographer.

We walked from the train station to the theater. Tartu is a hospitable town, very civilized. We kept seeing green student caps in the crowd. A transparent drizzle began.

"I need to buy some film," Zhbankov said.

We stopped by a pleasant little state-owned store. The salesman was making coffee on an electric hotplate. He was wearing a typical Estonian knitted jacket decorated with metallic buttons.

"Do you have any imported film?" Zhbankov asked.

The Estonian shook his head.

"Here we go . . ."

I became curious. "And where is the nearest store where we could get some?"

"Helsinki," the shopkeeper said without smiling.

"Fine," Zhbankov said. "I'll get some from the guys there who show up from the local Estonian *Forward!*"

The rain come down more heavily. We hurried to the theater. By the entrance there were crowds of people with umbrellas and plastic raincoats.

"What are they all carrying umbrellas for, like savages?" Zhbankov asked in surprise, stepping in a deep puddle.

"Not so loud," I said.

The Vanemuine Theater had been built comparatively recently. Marble staircases, spacious halls, reverberating echoes. Above its entrance hung a blue banner. (In Estonia, everyone likes blue banners.) "In Praise of the Former Prisoners of Fascist Concentration Camps!"

We found the Master of Ceremonies and introduced ourselves. He said, "The program goes like this. First, the emotional part—the meeting of old friends. Then the ceremonial assembly. At the end, the banquet. Incidentally, you are invited to attend."

"I should hope so," Zhbankov said.

People wearing decorations and medals were wandering through the halls. On the whole, they stood in groups of twos and threes, smoking and conversing quietly.

"Somehow I don't see too much emotion," Zhbankov said.

The Master of Ceremonies explained: "The prisoners have been meeting every year for close to twenty years. The emotional part will be over soon. The ceremonial part will last about an hour. Even less. After that comes the banquet . . ."

"With all its subsequent consequences," Zhbankov said, and he unexpectedly guffawed.

The M.C. winced.

"Excuse me," I said. "I need to talk to some of these people. To take some notes."

The M.C. called over a tall, solidly built man.

"Let me introduce you. Lazar Borisovich Slapak, construction engineer, former prisoner at Stutthof."

I also introduced myself.

"I was sent to Stutthof for anti-fascist activity and organizing escapes. Before that I had been imprisoned in Poland . . ."

Slapak spoke quietly and confidently. It was obvious that he was used to talking to journalists.

"You're probably interested in some unusual facts?" he asked.

I nodded.

"Come, let's sit down."

We sat on a sofa. Two other people joined us. One was a comparatively young man in a military tunic, the other a sad old man with only one arm. The M.C. supplied their names: Valton and Gurchenko.

Slapak waited for silence and then continued. "Organizing escapes necessitated having certain resources at our disposal. We had to think about getting together some money. And, imagine this, we actually found a way. I played chess, not badly either. And the camp commandant happened to be a passionate chess enthusiast. They decided to organize a match. A prize was set: eighty marks. My comrades rooted for me with everything they had. I won seven games out of ten. The commandant said, 'Damn!' and paid up."

"Interesting," the one-armed man interrupted. "Very interesting." Till then the old man had been silent. I noted down his name: Gurchenko.

"What's the matter, comrade?" Slapak asked.

"I would say you didn't spend your time badly . . ."

"Which is to say?" The construction engineer smiled tensely.

"You should try going to Socialist Mordovia for three years," the old man continued.

One could see that he was slightly drunk.

"And where were you imprisoned, comrade?" The M.C. put in quickly. "Dachau? Auschwitz?"

"I was imprisoned in Mordovia," Gurchenko answered, "and in Kazakhstan. I spent twenty years out there as a former prisoner of war."

"And do you think I wasn't imprisoned?" said the construction engineer, taking offense. "Both my kidneys were all beat up! Have you heard of the Socialist Republic of Komi? Of Yosser? Veslyana? Ropcha?"

"I've heard of them," said the younger man in the military jacket, keeping the conversation going. "I came down with meningitis in a transit prison in Ropcha. I was just a kid when I was first taken prisoner by the Germans. They sent me to a camp, even though I was too young for the draft, and hadn't taken part in propaganda activities. It was terribly unfair. I didn't like it in the concentration camp. The fascists starved us to death. Besides that, there were no women in the camp."

"And how did you manage to get to Ropcha?" the one-armed man asked maliciously.

"Very simple. We were liberated by the French. I found myself in Paris. I rushed to the Soviet embassy. They got together about eight hundred of us. Put us on a train. And sent us to the East. We kept going, going . . . We pass Moscow, then the Urals . . ."

"Smile, everyone!" Zhbankov said. "Attention! I'm taking a photograph!"

"Listen," I said. "You haven't even got any film in there."

"That's not important," Zhbankov said. "We need a little détente in the atmosphere in here."

The M.C. was also getting upset. He stood up and clapped his hands together loudly.

"Comrade Prisoners, please pass into the hall!"

The ceremonial part lasted all of twenty minutes. The M.C. himself spoke longer than anyone else. At the end he said, "We shall always remain prisoners of fascism. For that which we lived through shall never be forgotten."

"Was he a prisoner of war too?" I asked Gurchenko.

"That creep from the theater?" the old man answered. "He was appointed by the Party Committee. This is the fourth year he's been performing here. He should try going to Socialist Mordovia for three years . . . Working on the logging crew . . ."

At that moment they opened the doors of the banquet hall. We took a table by the window. Zhbankov pulled over two more chairs. Then he poured out the vodka.

"Let's drink without toasts for all the best!" Slapak proposed.

We drank silently. Zhbankov immediately poured the next round. Valton tried to tell me the rest of his story.

"I was a cabin boy on a merchant marine ship. The Germans made a mistake. They threw me in prison for no reason. I wasn't in the Navy. I worked on a merchant ship. But they went and put me in prison. For no reason, actually . . ."

Valton seemed eager to prove his innocence. He all but declared his loyalty to the Germans.

"That's what Germans are like," Zhbankov said. "Adolf was their best friend. But Russians they look down on."

"And what should they love us for?" Gurchenko butted in. "For the brothel we've made out of Estonia?"

"A brothel isn't bad," Zhbankov said. "What's bad is that vodka's getting so expensive."

His face had begun to shine. The bottles simply flashed through his hands.

"Can I serve you some of the main course?" Slapak said, stooping over me.

Zhbankov politely touched his elbow. "I've been meaning to ask you. As they say, this is an indelicate question . . . I beg your pardon, but what nation would you belong to?"

Barely noticeably, Slapak became guarded. Then he answered firmly and confidently. He spoke with the voice of a man who had nothing to hide: "I belong to the Jewish nation. And you, excuse me, what would your nation be?"

Zhbankov got somewhat flustered. He speared a slippery marinated mushroom. "Mine would be the Russian . . . Jewish nation," he said amicably.

At this point the one-armed Gurchenko turned to Slapak. "Don't be upset, lad," he said. "If you're a Jew, so you're a Jew. There's nothing so terrible about it. I lived in Kazakhstan for four years. The Kazakhs are a hundred times worse."

We drank again. Zhbankov began an animated conversation with Gurchenko. His speech became more and more off-color.

Gradually the banquet hall filled with its characteristic rumble. Glasses and forks clattered. Someone turned on the radio. Mighty chords rang out:

> . . . *The country is at war,*
> *A sacred war . . .*

"Hey! Who's the closest to that thing? Cut out the noise!" Zhbankov yelled.

"Leave it," I said. "We need to drown out your cursing."

"The truth can't be drowned out!" Gurchenko shouted unexpectedly.

Zhbankov stood up and headed for the radio. Just at that moment, I noticed a group of schoolchildren in Pioneer uniforms. They were making their way awkwardly between the tables Evidently they had been delayed by the downpour. The Pioneers carried an enormous basket of flowers.

Misha ran into them on his way to the radio. His appearance was certainly picturesque. His eyes glittered with excitement. His tie lay on his shoulder.

Among the former concentration camp inmates, Zhbankov distinguished himself by his emaciation and tragic aspect.

The Pioneers halted. Zhbankov stood before them, shifting from foot to foot in confusion. A skinny boy wearing a crimson tie raised his hand. Someone shut off the radio.

In the silence that had fallen, the high-pitched voice of the child rang out:

"Eternal praise to the heroes!"

And then, three times: "Praise them! Praise them! Praise them!"

Frightened, Zhbankov clutched the basket of flowers to his chest.

After a pause, he yelled, "Hurrah!"

An unimaginable din arose in the hall. Someone was already dragging props out of boxes. Someone was dancing the kazatski with a fake dagger between his teeth.

Zhbankov was photographed by the young reporters from the local newspaper. His crimson face sank into green. He returned to our table. Hoisted the basket onto the windowsill.

Gurchenko lifted his head slightly. Then he collapsed again onto a dish of potatoes.

I pulled my chair over to Zhbankov.

"An elegant bouquet you have there," I said.

"It's not a bouquet," Zhbankov answered mournfully, "it's a funeral wreath!"

On this tragic note I said farewell to journalism. Enough!

THE COMPROMISE

• • •

My first cousin, who has been convicted twice (once for unpremeditated manslaughter), often says to me:

"Take up some useful kind of work. Aren't you ashamed of what you do?"

"You're a fine one to lecture me!"

"All I did was kill a man," my cousin says, "and try to burn his body. But you!"